GW01425117

CHINESE CLASSICS

STRANGE TALES FROM THE LIAOZHAI STUDIO

Pu Songling

Retold by Wang Guozhen

China Intercontinental Press

图书在版编目（CIP）数据

聊斋志异故事：英文 / （清）蒲松龄著；王国振译. -- 北京：
五洲传播出版社，2016.12
（中国经典名著故事）
ISBN 978-7-5085-3526-5

Ⅰ. ①聊… Ⅱ. ①蒲… ②王… Ⅲ. ①笔记小说－中国－清代－英文 Ⅳ.
①I242.1

中国版本图书馆CIP数据核字(2016)第211542号

聊斋志异故事

出 版 人：荆孝敏
英文改编：王国振
责任编辑：苏 谦
设计总监：闫志杰
封面设计：谢金宝
插画设计：蒋 琼
内文制作：杨 山

出版发行：五洲传播出版社
地 址：北京市海淀区北三环中路31号生产力大楼B座7层
邮 编：100088
发行电话：010-82005927，010-82007837
网 址：http://www.cicc.org.cn http://www.thatsbooks.com
印 刷：北京浙京印刷有限公司
开 本：889×1194mm 1/32
印 张：10.25
版 次：2017年3月第1版第1次印刷
定 价：88.00元

CONTENTS

TALE 1

The Taoist Priest of Laoshan Mountain

There used to be a scholar named Wang who was the seventh child in an official's family. When he heard there were immortals up on Laoshan Mountain, he decided to go and visit them.

He climbed up to a mountain peak and there he found a Taoist temple in very quiet surroundings. A Taoist sat on the dais, his white hair reaching down to his shoulders.

Wang the Seventh begged to be his student.

The Taoist said, "I am afraid you are spoiled and lazy. You can't stand hardship."

"Oh," Wang the Seventh said. "But I can!"

The Taoist had many students, and Wang the Seventh bowed respectfully to each and every one of them and so they agreed to let him stay.

Coming back one evening from gathering firewood, he saw the Priest and two men drinking wine together.

Then one of the guests said, "This has been a wonderful evening. Won't you see me off to the Moon Palace?"

And then and there, the three, still in their seats, glided right into the moon. They could be seen drinking merrily in the moon, their eyebrows and bears as clear as ever, just as though reflected in mirror.

Another month went by. The hard life had become just too much for him. Besides, the Taoist wasn't teaching him any arts. Wang the Seventh felt he couldn't wait any longer, so he went to say goodbye to the Taoist.

The Taoist smiled and said, "I said at the beginning you wouldn't be able to stand the hardship. Now you've proven me right. Tomorrow, you can go."

Wang the Seventh said, "I've worked for so long. Could you please teach me some little magic trick so my stay here won't all have been for nothing."

The Taoist, smiling, taught him the rhyme and told him to go through the wall.

Wang the Seventh took a few steps backward and then ran at the wall. When he got there, i5t was like running into empty space; there seemed to be nothing in his way. When he looked back, he found himself outside the wall.

The Taoist said to him, "After you get back home, you must be prudent and avoid evil. Otherwise, the magic won't work."

Upon home, Wang the Seventh boasted he had met all immortals, and now, not even

the thickest wall could prevent him from passing through. His wife wouldn't believe him. So, he stepped back a few steps and then charged towards the wall. He bumped his head and fell to the ground. When his wife helped him up, she saw a bump as big as an egg on his forehead.

TALE 2

The Snakeman

A man living in East Prefecture was a snake-tamer by profession. At one point, he reared two green snakes, the bigger he called Big Green, and the smaller one, Second Green. The latter had several red spots on its forehead and was particularly clever. It weaved about and danced just the way the tamer wanted. The tamer loved it far more than any other snake in his possession. A year later, Big Green died. The tamer wanted to find another snake to take its place but never got to it.

Once, while in the mountains, he spent the night in a temple. When morning came, he opened his bamboo basket only to find that Second Green had disappeared. Feeling very sad, he looked everywhere for it, calling the snake by name. But it was not to be found. In the past, whenever they passed through an area overthrown with grass, the tamer would let Second Green out of the basket to go free for a while, and it would always come back. So this time, he again pinned his hopes on a similar return. He sat in the temple and waited until the sun was high. Then, he gave up hope and went on his way, feeling very downcast.

He had gone only a little way from the temple when he heard a hissing sound corning from a pile of firewood. Astonished, the snake-tamer stopped. Sure enough, it was Second Green. The man was beside himself with joy, as though he had found a treasure. He laid down his bag at the corner of the road. Second Green stopped, too, and the tamer spied another little snake close behind him. The tamer caressed Second Green and said, "I thought you'd never come back. Did you bring this little one along?" He took out some feed for Second Green, and for the little one as well. But the little snake froze and dared not take the food. Then Second Green took the food in its mouth and fed it to the little one, just as the host at a dinner would serve his guest. After that, the little snake ate what the tamer offered it. When they had finished, it followed Second Green into the Basket. The snake-tamer took it back home to train. It learned to weave about and to advance and retreat just as required and was soon no different from Second Green. So it was given the name Little Green. With the two, the tamer travelled far and wide, displaying his snake-trainer's skills and made no small amount of money from it.

Usually, the standard size of a snake for a tamer is about two feet. When it gets too large, it becomes too heavy and bulky and must be replaced. As Second Green was particularly tame, the snake-man was reluctant to replace it as soon as it surpassed the standard length but waited two or three years until it grew to more than three feet long. By then, when it coiled up, it occupied the whole basket. So the man decided to release it. One day, he came to Zibo's East Mountain. He took out some extra good feed and fed it to Second Green. Then, after giving it his blessing, he let it go. But after only a little while, Second Green returned. It lingered around the basket. The tamer waved for it to go away, saying, "Go on! Get going! There's an end to all banquets. From now on, you can live in seclusion in the mountain valleys and you will turn into a holy dragon. The bamboo basket can't keep you forever." At this, Second Green departed, and the snakeman watched it leave. But before long, it came back again and this time, nothing could keep it away. It kept knocking its head against the basket. Inside, Little Green appeared restless, too. The man suddenly realized, "Perhaps it wants to say goodbye to Little Green." So he opened the basket. Little Green emerged immediately and the two snakes put their heads together, throwing out their tongues, as though speaking to each other. Then the two slithered away together, twisting and turning as they went. Just when the tamer began to doubt if Little Green would come clack, the snake returned, alone. It slid into the basket and settled down.

From then on, wherever he went, the snakeman looked around for a good snake but never found one unique enough for him. Meanwhile, Little Green was growing bigger and bigger until it could no longer perform. He did find a young snake, once, which was quite easy to tame. Nevertheless, it could not compare with Little Green who had by now grown to be as thick as a child's upper arm.

In the beginning, the firewood cutters often caught sight Second Green in the mountains. But as the years passed, Second Green grew to be many feet long and as big as a large bowl. It started to chase after passers-by. People began to warn each other so that no one dared to wander on that part of the mountain any more. One day, the snakeman came that way. As he was walking along, a huge snake suddenly darted out from nowhere, moving as fast as lightning. The man was awfully frightened and ran for his life. The snake followed in hot pursuit. The tamer looked back and saw that the snake had just about caught up with him. Then, he caught sight of the red spots on the snake's forehead. It was Second Green! He laid down his shoulder-pole and baskets and called out to the snake, "Second Green! Second Green!" Right away, the snake stopped in its tracks, raised its head for quite a while, and then leaped onto the snakeman's body, coiling around him as it did in the old days during performances. The tamer knew Second Green had no ill intentions, but it had grown so big and heavy that he found it hard to bear its weight. He fell to the ground and cried out and prayed. Only then did Second Green relax its grip. It knocked its head against the basket many times. Knowing what that meant, the tamer opened the basket and let out Little Green. The two snakes wrapped themselves around each other for a long time before they separated.

The snakeman then said to Little Green, "I have long thought of letting you leave. Now you have your companion." And turning to Second Green, he said, "You brought Little Green here, now you can take it back. And one other thing, you don't lack food in the mountains, so don't harass people passing by, lest you violate the laws of Heaven and anger the gods." The two snakes lowered their heads, apparently taking in his admonition. Then, they suddenly lifted their bodies and sailed away, the big one in front, the little one behind. As they did so the grass and bushes moved to either side to make way. The snakeman stood there and watched them disappear into the distance. Ever since then, people have trekked all over the East Mountain as usual. No one knows where the two snakes went.

The Chronicler of the Tales had this to say, Snakes are, after all, stupid animals, and yet they cherish love and friendship for each other, and moreover, are willing to accept advice without feeling offended. What I find strange is that some people appear to be human, and yet they are always trying to hit a person when he's down even if the victim is a friend of long standing or a master to whom they owe much. Or, rather than heed the advice of a friend, they go into a rage and even regard him as an enemy. Such people should feel ashamed before Second Green and Little Green.

TALE 3

Hacking the Boa

Two brothers surnamed Hu from Hutian Village walked into a deep mountain ravine. There they came upon a huge boa. As the elder brother was walking in front, the boa caught him first. At first, the frightened younger brother was going to run away, but when he saw that the boa had swallowed part of his brother, he was so enraged that he lifted the ax he used for cutting firewood and hacked away at the boa's head. Although wounded in the head, the boa was still straggling to swallow the rest of its prey. It had already swallowed the head. Luckily, it was now having difficulty getting the shoulders into its mouth. Frantic and for lack of a better way, the younger brother grasped his elder brother's feet. After a tug-of-war with the boa, he managed to pull his brother out of the boa's mouth. Wounded, the boa left. The younger brother examined his brother's wounds and found that he had lost his nose and ears and was on the verge of death. He quickly lifted his brother on his back and went home, stopping more than a dozen times to catch his breath. The elder brother gradually recovered after receiving medical treatment and recuperating for more than half a year. Even today, you can still see scars on his face and holes where his nose and ears used to be.

Well, even among uneducated farmers, there are people like the younger brother who cherish brotherly love! Someone said, "The boa didn't kill the elder brother because it was moved by the younger brother's loyalty." Perhaps, that's true!

TALE 4
The Dog Adulterer

A merchant from Yidu in Shandong Province was often away from home for a year on end, living in some other town. So his wife taught their white dog to copulate with her. Gradually, the dog became accustomed to doing this. One day, the merchant returned. While he was in bed with his wife, the white dog suddenly came in. It jumped onto the bed and bit the merchant to death. Eventually, the incident leaked out and the neighbors felt indignant on the merchant's behalf. They reported the case to the local authorities, and the woman was arrested. Since she refused to admit her crime, she was thrown into prison. Then the judge ordered the white dog to be bound and brought in, and subsequently, called for the woman. As soon as the dog saw her, he dashed forth, tore at her clothes and poised for copulation. The woman had nothing left to say in her own defence. The judge ordered two of his men to take the two to the governor's headquarters, one escorting the woman and the other the dog. On their way, some people wanted to witness the white dog having sex with the woman, so they pooled some money to bribe the two escorts. The escorts then led the dog to the woman to let them perform the act. Whenever they stopped to do that, they would draw crowds of several hundred people. The two escorts made quite a lot of money as a result. In the end, both the woman and the dog were put to death by a slow process.

TALE 5

Wild Dogs

The uprising in Qixia County, Shandong Province, led by Yu Qi resulted in the killing of countless people. A villager by the name of Li Hualong was trying to steal back into the village from the hills when he came upon a unit of government soldiers on the march. Fearing that he might be mistaken for a rebel and be killed too, like destroying the jade along with the stone, he tried to find a place to hide himself, but couldn't. Desperate, he lay down stiff among the corpses, pretending to be one of them. Even after the soldiers had gone by, he still didn't dare to get up right away. Suddenly, he saw the corpses, without head or limbs, rise one by one; almost like a forest they stood. One of the corpses, whose broken head was still hanging from its shoulder, was mumbling, "What if the wild dogs come along?" And the group of corpses echoed uniformly, "What shall we do then!" After a while, they fell to the ground again and all was quiet.

Li Hualong, still quivering with fear, was just about to pick himself up from the ground when he saw a monster with the head of an animal and the body of a human approach. He bit open the heads of the corpses and, one by one, sucked out the brains. Li was so frightened that he hid his head under a corpse. The monster came over and pushed at his shoulder in an attempt to get to his head. Li held to his position with all his might, so that the monster could not reach his head. But then the monster pushed the corpse above him to one side and Li Hualong's head was exposed. Frightened to the extreme, he felt for a bowl-size rock that lay beneath his waist and held it tightly in his band. When the monster bent down to bite him, he leapt up and, with a loud cry, raised the rock and hit hard at the monster's head. It struck the monster's mouth. Hooting like an owl, the monster ran away, its hand on the wound, spitting blood on the way. Li went up for a closer look. He found two four-inch-long teeth in the pool of blood, crooked in the middle and sharp at the ends. He took them home and showed them to the others, but no one knew what monster it could have been.

TALE 6

Reincarnated Three Times

L iu, a juren, remembered things from his former lives and confided in my deceased cousin, Pu Wenfen, as they both became juren in the same year.

Liu had started out as a court official and had performed many misdeeds during his lifetime. After he died at the age of sixty-two and was taken to see the King of Hell, the latter greeted him in the traditional manner of the village, offering him a seat and serving him tea. From the corner of his eye, Liu saw that the tea in the king's cup was clear and transparent, whereas that in his cup looked cloudy, like unstrained wine. He was overcome by suspicion. Could this be a magic potion? So when the King of Hell turned his head aside, he quickly picked up the cup and poured the tea down the corner of the table, pretending he had drunk it all. After a while, when the king had checked the records of Liu's past misconducts, he was very angry and ordered the little demons to drag Liu from his seat and, as penalty, make him a horse in his next life. Immediately, ferocious-looking demons appeared, bound him and took him away.

They came to a house. The threshold was so high Liu found it hard to cross. Just as he hesitated, the demon whacked him with his hatchet. It was so painful that he jumped and the next thing he knew, he was lying in a stable. He could hear somebody say, "The black horse has given birth to a pony. It's a male." Liu knew in his heart what it was all about, but he just couldn't speak. He felt very hungry. Faced with no other alternative, he tried to reach beneath the mother horse for some milk.

Four or five years passed and Liu had grown into a big, tall steed. But he was very much afraid of the horsewhip and would run for his life every time he saw it. When the master rode him, he always put padding under the saddle, loosened the rein and trod along slowly, so it wasn't too bad. But when the servants or the groom rode him, they never used padding and would kick his belly with their heels which made it extremely painful. Finally, he got so mad that he refused to eat for three days and died.

So once again, he was back in hell. The King of Hell checked with the life-and-death book and found that Liu had not finished serving his term. He reprimanded Liu for intentionally escaping punishment. He was condemned to have his skin peeled off and be a dog in his next life. Liu was full of remorse. He did not want to go, but a group of demons gave him a thorough beating which hurt so much that he scurried off to the countryside. He thought to himself, "Why, it's better to die than to live like this." So he jumped down from the edge of a precipice and fell to the ground below. Unable to get up, he took a look at himself and found he was curled up in a cave with a female dog licking him and caring for him. He realized that he had returned to the world of mortals.

When he had grown a little bigger, he recognized urine as something dirty. Although he thought it smelled rather good, he knew in his heart he must never taste it. When as a dog he was one year old, he thought of killing himself again, being so angry with his lot. But he feared the King of Hell would charge him again with intentionally evading punishment. Besides, the master treated him well and would not slaughter him. So what he did was to bite off a big chunk of flesh from the master's leg. Infuriated, the master beat him to death with a stick.

Back in hell, the king checked to find out why he was dead. He was very angered by Liu's disobedience and called on his followers to give Liu several hundred lashes and then send him back to the world of mortals as a snake. Thus, Liu was shut up in a dark room where he could not see the light of day. It was so dull that he crawled up along the wall and made a hole in the roof. Out in the open, he saw that he was lying in a grass thicket and had actually turned into a snake. From then he made up his mind never to injure a living thing and ate only fruits from the trees to stay his hunger.

Another year or so passed. He couldn't kill himself, much as he wanted to. Nor could he die by injuring others. He racked his brains to think of a safe way to die, but was unsuccessful. One day, he was curled up in the grass by the roadside when he heard a cart coming his way. He suddenly thrust himself forward and lay stretched out across the road. The cart rolled right over him, cutting him in half. The King of Hell was surprised by his fast return. So he crouched on the ground and revealed his wish. Since he had been killed this time without committing any crime, the king pardoned him. He said he could stay in hell until his term was up and then return to the world as a man. That's how Liu, the juren, came to be.

Liu knew how to talk at birth and could recite essays and books after one reading. He won the title of juren in the first year of the reign of Tianqi (1621) towards the end of the Ming Dynasty. He often admonished others to put a thick padding under the saddle when they went horseback-riding and that pressing one's heels against the horse's belly is worse than lashing it with a whip.

TALE 7
Wang Lan

A man named Wang Lan, who lived in Lijing County, in Shandong Province, suddenly died. When the King of Hell checked the Life and Death Book, he found that one of the little demons had marked the wrong soul. So he ordered the little demon to send Wang Lan back to the mortals. But Wang Lan's body had already decayed. Fearing that the King of Hell might punish him for his mistake, the little demon said to Wang Lan, "It is very painful for a human to turn into a ghost, but for a ghost to turn into an immortal, that's a very happy experience. To be happy is enough. Why bother to be revived from death?" Wang Lan thought there was something to what he said. The little demon went on, "There is a fox here which has been successful in making immortality pills. If you steal and eat one, your soul will stay with you forever. Wherever you go, you will get what you want. Would you like to do that?" Wang Lan said, "Yes."

The little demon led Wang Lan into a grand villa which had many tall buildings and pavilions but was very quiet, without a single person in sight. Only a lone fox was there, looking up at the moon in the sky. When it breathed out, it emitted a ball-like pill from its mouth which shot up right into the moon. When it breathed in, the pill would drop from the moon and the fox would catch it with his mouth. This process was repeated over and over again. The little demon hid himself beside the fox so that when it spat out the pill, he quickly caught it with his hand and gave it to Wang Lan to swallow. Surprised, the fox turned to face them angrily, but when it saw there were two of them, it shrank back and slipped away, grumbling. Wang Lan said goodbye to the little demon and went home. When his wife and children saw him, they were scared out of their wits and avoided him. Only when Wang Lan had told them the whole process did they come up to him. From then on, life went on as usual in the Wang family.

Wang Lan had a friend by the name of Zhang. When he heard the news, he came to call on Wang. After an exchange of greetings, Wang Lan said to Zhang, "My family and yours have always been poor. Now I have a way of getting rich. Can you go traveling with me?" Zhang said yes. Wang said, "I can cure a person of his illness without using medicine. I can tell a person's fortune without resorting to divination. I would like to appear as myself but fear that those who recognize me would be shocked. So I thought of attaching my soul to your body, do you agree?" Zhang said he did. So they got ready and set out that very day.

They came to a place west of the mountain where they happened upon an emergency case, the daughter of a rich family was in a coma. No matter what medicine she took or how they prayed to avoid this misfortune and disaster, nothing worked. Zhang walked into the house and boasted that he had a magic cure. Now the rich man had only this one daughter whom he adored and was willing to give one thousand taels of silver to anyone who could cure her. Zhang said he must first have a look at the patient, so he followed the father into the inner chamber where the girl was lying in bed, her eyes closed. Zhang moved the quilt aside and touched her body. She remained unconscious and did not respond. Wang Lan said to Zhang on the side, "This shows she has lost her soul. I must go and find it and bring it back." So Zhang said to the rich man, "Although the situation is critical, there is still hope." The rich man asked, "What medicine is needed?" Zhang replied, "There's no need to use any medicine. Your daughter's soul has left her. I have already sent someone to find it."

About an hour later, Wang Lan suddenly returned, saying he had found the soul and brought it back. Zhang asked the rich man to let him into the chamber again. He again moved his hand softly over the girl's body. After a while, the girl stretched her arms and suddenly opened her eyes. Overjoyed, the rich man caressed his daughter and asked her many questions. The girl said, "I was playing in the garden when I saw a young man shooting at birds with a slingshot, followed by several men leading horses. I immediately tried to hide myself, but they wouldn't let me get away. The young man gave me his slingshot and taught me how to use it. I was very embarrassed and was scolding him when he pulled me onto his horse and together we galloped off. He laughed and said, "I am happy to have you to play with. Don't be shy." We went like that for several miles and started climbing the mountain, while I shouted and cursed all the way. He got so angry that he pushed me off the horse onto the roadside. I wanted to come home but didn't know the way. Just then, a man came along. He grabbed my arm and dragged me along. We were going so fast we were flying. In the twinkling of an eye, I was home. I feel as though I'd just awakened from a dream." The rich man thought it sounded quite fantastic and, as promised, gave Zhang one thousand taels of silver.

That night, Wang Lan proposed to Zhang that they keep two

hundred taels of the silver to cover traveling expenses. The rest he took back home. He gave it to his son, bidding him to give three hundred taels to Zhang's wife, and then hurried back. The next day, when they bade farewell to the rich man, the latter wondered where they could have hidden the silver. He presented Zhang with lots of gifts and saw him off.

A few days later, while in the suburbs, Zhang met a man from his hometown named He Chai. He Chai was a drunkard and a gambler. He did no work and was extremely poor. He had heard that Zhang had mastered some strange magic and had profited immensely from it, so he came to look for him. Wang Lan advised Zhang to give him a little bit of silver and send him home. But He Chai kept to his old ways. Within ten days, he had lost all the money that Zhang had given him. He came to see Zhang again. This Wang Lan had expected. He said to Zhang, "He Chai is a good-for-nothing, but very presumptuous and unrestrained. You mustn't have too much to do with him. Why don't you give him some money and tell him to go away? This way, even if some misfortune falls, you won't be too involved." Sure enough, He Chai showed up again a day later. He insisted on keeping Zhang company. Zhang said to him, "I knew long ago that you would come again. All day long, you do nothing but drink and gamble. Even if you had a thousand taels of silver, would it be enough to fill this bottomless pit? If you can really mend your ways, I'll give you a hundred taels of silver." He Chai promised he would start anew, whereupon Zhang poured out all the silver from his bag and gave it to He Chai. But after he left Zhang, He Chai gambled with even more abandon, thinking he was now rich. On top of that, he frequented the brothels, squandering money like water. This aroused the suspicion of the police who arrested him and took him to the local authorities. After a severe beating and other forms of torture, he confessed to where the silver had come from. Then the magistrate ordered his men to go and arrest Zhang, taking He Chai with them. A few days later, He Chai died on the road on account of the severe wounds inflicted on him. Still not resigned to leaving Zhang alone, he attached his spirit to Zhang, and that's how he became acquainted with Wang Lan.

One day, while drinking together on a mound, He Chai got thoroughly besotted. He shouted and screamed wildly; nothing Wang Lan said could stop him. An imperial emissary, sent from the nation's capital on an inspection tour of the area, happened to pass by. When he heard the screaming, he searched and found Zhang, who for fear of punishment, confessed the whole truth. Angered by what he heard, the emissary gave Zhang a good beating and then wrote an official note to the gods. That night, he dreamt that a god in gold armor told him, "We have checked and found that Wang Lan died innocent and is now a ghost-spirit. Treating patients is an act of benevolence and should therefore not be regarded as a demonic act. I have brought you an order from the Heavenly King, conferring on Wang Lan the post of Minister in Charge of Street-Cleaning. He Chai is evil and dissipated. For that he has been sentenced to exile on Tiewei Mountain. As for Zhang, he is found not guilty and should be pardoned." When the emissary woke up, he was struck with amazement. So he set Zhang free. Zhang put his things together and went home. He still had several hundred taels of silver in his pocket. With all reverence, he gave half of it to the Wang family. From then on, Wang Lan's children and grandchildren lived a prosperous life.

TALE 8

Flood

In the 21st year of the reign of the Qing Emperor Kangxi (1682), drought hit Shandong Province, lasting from spring to summer. The fields were cracked and even the grass did not grow. On June 13, light rain fell and some people began to sow millet. On June 18, a heavy rain fell and people began to sow beans. One day, an old man living in Shimen Village, seeing two buffaloes fighting atop a hill at sunset, told his fellow villagers, "A flood is imminent!" Then he moved his family to another place. The villagers thought the old man was crazy. Not long after, there was a downpour that kept on for all night. The water was a few feet deep, and all the houses were immersed in water. A farmer and his wife helped his mother rush to higher ground, leaving behind his two sons. When he got to the high place he turned around to look at his village; there was nothing but an expanse of water. He could do nothing about his two sons. When the water receded, he went back to the village, which was now in ruins. He got into his house and saw that it was intact. The two children were sitting on the bed, frolicking with each other as if nothing had happened. People said that this was the result of the couple's filially dutiful conduct. This happened on June 22.

In the 24th year of the reign of the Emperor Kangxi (1685), an earthquake struck Pingyang. Seven or eight people out of ten died. The whole city was leveled. The only house intact belonged to a filial son. Havoc and calamities frequently visit this vast world. But only the people who cling to filial duties are protected from the disasters. Who can say that Heaven is blind or doesn't see the difference between white and black?

TALE 9

A Man in Zhucheng

Sun Jingxia, proctor of Zhucheng County, once told a story, A man in Zhucheng County was wounded by roving bandits. His head was cut off and hung in front of his chest. After the bandits withdrew, his family found his body and was going to bury it when a weak gasping sound was heard. The family members took a careful look and found that the head was still linked to the body by the throat. They carried the wounded man home, with one man holding up the head. The next day, the man began to groan and the family members fed him a little food with chopsticks and a spoon. Half a year passed and the man recovered his health. Who would have thought it?

A dozen more years passed. The man was talking with a few of his friends one day. One of the friends told a joke and all burst out laughing. The man was very worked up and clapped his hand merrily. With his body rocking back and forth, the sword-wrought scar around his neck suddenly burst and the head fell off to the ground and blood spilled out from his body. People looked at him and found he was already dead. His father wanted to sue the joke teller. The matter was not settled until after the persons involved gathered some money, gave it to the father of the dead man, asked his pardon and had the dead buried with some more money.

This writer says, Hearty laughter could even sever one's head. Isn't that itself an unprecedented joke? The head was linked to the neck by only a piece of flesh but the man was still alive. And he remained alive a dozen years, until a joke caused his death. Doesn't that suggest that the friends of the dead had been indebted to the dead man in their previous incarnations?

TALE 10
Treasury Ward

During the reign of Ming Emperor Wanli, Zhang Hua-dong of Zouping County, in Shandong Province, was a court official. He had accepted an order from the emperor to offer sacrifices on sacred Mount Hengshan, which was situated in southern Hunan Province. On his way south, he was crossing Jiangsu and Anhui provinces. One day, he planned to stay in a post hostel for the night. His servant reported to him, "There is a monster in the post hostel. We could get in trouble if we stay there." Zhang did not listen. At midnight, Zhang still sat upright in the hostel, in full dress and holding his sword. Presently, he heard footsteps. Looking up, he saw an old man with gray hair, wearing a black felt hat and a black waist belt. Zhang felt strange and asked the intruder who he was. The old man knelt down and saluted him, saying, "I'm the treasury warden here and have been taking care of your wealth for a long time. Now that you yourself are here, I can free myself of the task." Zhang asked him, "How much wealth is there?" The old man answered, "23,500 taels of silver." Fearing that it would be burdensome to travel with such a large amount of silver, Zhang made an agreement with the old man that he would take charge of the wealth on his way back from Mount Hengshan. The old man nodded his head, agreed and left.

In the south, Zhang received generous gifts. On his way back, he stayed again at the hostel, and the old man came to see him again. When Zhang asked about the wealth in the treasury, the old man, answered, "The silver has been allotted to Liangdong for soldiers' pay and provisions." Zhang wondered why he contradicted himself. The old man said, "The wealth in one's life is a fixed figure, not one tael more or less. Your Excellency, your southern tour already gained you what you deserve. Why are you still asking for more?" After this, he turned around and walked off. Zhang proceeded to calculate what he had received as gifts in the south and found that the amount tallied with the amount the old man had told him. He could say nothing but sighed that everyone's fate was preset and one should not desire anything more.

TALE 11

Examination for the
Post of City God

One day, Sung Tao was lying down from indisposition when an official messenger arrived, leading a horse with a white forehead to summon him to the imperial examination.

Song asked why there should be this hurry. The messenger did not reply to this, but pressed so earnestly that at length Song roused himself, and getting upon the horse rode with him.

They reached a town, which resembled the capital of a prince. They then entered the Prefect's apartments which were beautifully decorated. There they found some 10 officials sitting at the upper end, all strangers to Song, with the exception of one whom he recognized to be the God of War.

On the table were writing materials for each, and suddenly down flew a piece of paper with a theme on it, consisting of the following eight words, "One man, two men; by intention, without intention."

When Song had finished his essay, he took it into the hall. It contained the following passage, "Those who are virtuous by intention, though virtuous, shall not be rewarded. Those who are wicked without intention, though wicked, shall receive no punishment."

The presiding deities praised this sentiment very much, and called Song to come forward, "A Guardian Angel is wanted in Hunan. Go you and take up the appointment."

Song no sooner heard this than he bowed his head and wept, saying, "Unworthy though I am of the honor you have conferred upon me, I should not venture to decline it but that my aged mother has reached her seventh decade, and there is no one now to take care of her. I pray you let me wait until she has fulfilled her destiny, when I will hold myself at your disposal."

Thereupon one of the deities, who seemed to be the chief, gave instructions to search out his mother's term of life, and a long-bearded attendant forthwith brought in the Book of Fate.

Nine years afterwards, Song's mother, in accordance with fate, passed from this life; and when the funeral obsequies were over, her son, having first purified himself, entered into his chamber and died also.

Now his wife's family lived within the city, near the western gate; and all of a sudden they beheld Song, accompanied by numerous chariots and horses with carved trappings and red-tasselled bits, enter into the hall, make an obeisance, and depart.

They were very much disconcerted at this, not knowing that he had become a spirit, and rushed out into the village to make inquiries, when they heard he was already dead.

Song had an account of his adventure written by himself; but unfortunately after the insurrection it was not to be found. This is only an outline of the story.

TALE 12
Talking Eye Pupils

One day, a scholar, named Fang Tong, was strolling about outside the city of Chang'an when he saw a small carriage with red curtains and an embroidered awning, followed by a crowd of waiting-maids on horseback, one of whom was exceedingly pretty, and riding on a small palfrey.

Fang noticed that the carriage curtain was partly open, and inside he beheld a beautifully dressed girl of about 16, lovely beyond anything he had ever seen. Dazzled by the sight, he could not take his eyes off her; and, now before, now behind, he followed the carriage for many a mile.

The young lady call out to her maid, and, when the latter came alongside, say to her, "Let down the screen for me. Who is this rude fellow that keeps on staring so?"

The maid accordingly let down the screen, and looking angrily at Fang said to him, "This is the bride of the Seventh Prince in the City of Immortals going home to see her parents, and no village girl that you should stare at her thus."

Then taking a handful of dust, she threw it at him and blinded him. He rubbed his eyes and looked round, but the carriage and horses were gone.

This frightened him, and he went off home, feeling very uncomfortable about the eyes.

He sent for a doctor to examine his eyes, and on the pupils was found a small film, which had increased by next morning, the eyes watering incessantly all the time. The film went on growing, and in a few days was as thick as a cash. On the right pupil there came a kind of spiral, and as no medicine was of any avail, the sufferer gave himself up to grief and wished for death.

One day at the end of that year, he heard a small voice, about as loud as a fly's, calling out from his left eye, "It's horridly dark in here." To this he heard a reply from the right eye, saying, "Let us go out for a stroll, and cheer ourselves up a bit."

Then he felt a wriggling in his nose which made it itch, just as if something was going out of each of the nostrils; and after a while he felt it again as if going the other way. Afterward she heard a voice from one eye say, "I hadn't seen the garden for a long time, the flowers are all withered and dead."

Hearing these words, Fang at once asked his wife why she had let the flowers die. She inquired how he knew they were dead, and when he told her to go out to see, and found them actually withered away.

Days later, Fang heard from the left eye, "This roundabout road is not at all convenient. It would be as well for us to make a door."

To this the right eye answered, "My wall is too thick, it wouldn't be an easy job."

"I'll try and open mine," said the left eye, "and then it will do for both of us."

Whereupon Fang felt a Bain in his left eye as if something

was being split, and in a moment he found he could see the tables and chairs in the room. He was delighted at this and told his wife, who examined his eye and discovered an opening in the film, through which she could see the black pupil shining out beneath, the eyeball itself looking like a cracked pepper-corn.

By next morning, the film had disappeared, and when his eye was closely examined it was observed to contain two pupils. The spiral on the right eye remained as before; and then they knew that the two pupils had taken up their abode in one eye. Further, although Fang was still blind of one eye, the sight of the other was better than that of the two together. From this time he was more careful of his behavior, and acquired in his part of the country the reputation of a virtuous man.

TALE 13

The Mural

Meng Longtan, a man from Jiangxi, was visiting the capital together with a man named Zhu. One day they happened to see a monastery with no spacious halls or meditation chambers, but only an old priest. On the east side were pictured a number of fairies, among whom was a young girl whose maiden tresses were not yet confined by the matron's knot. She was picking flowers and gently smiling, while her red lips seemed about to move, and the moisture of her eyes to overflow.

Mr. Zhu gazed for a long time without taking his eyes off her. Then, suddenly he felt himself floating in the air, and found himself passing through the wall where halls and pavilions stretched away one after another. An old priest was seen preaching, surrounded by a large crowd of listeners. Mr. Zhu mingled with the throng, and after a few moments perceived a gentle tug at his sleeve.

All of a sudden, Mr. Zhu saw the girl he missed very much and followed her to a small apartment. The young lady waved the flowers she had in her hand as though beckoning him to come on. He entered and they got married there.

One day, they heard a strange sound like the clanking of chains and the noise of angry discussion. They peeped out and saw a black-faced man clad in golden armour, carrying in his hands chains and whips, and surrounded by many girls.

"Any mortal is here concealed amongst you, denounce him at once, and lay not up sorrow for yourselves?" he asked the girls.

In her terror Zhu's wife asked her husband to hide himself under the bed. Shen then opened a small lattice in the wall and disappeared herself.

Lying under the bed, Mr. Zhu heard the voices of people going backwards and forwards outside.

On his part, Meng Longtan had noticed the sudden disappearance of his friend, and asked the priest where he was.

"He has gone to listen to the preaching of the Law," replied the priest.

The old priest tapped his finger on the wall and called out, "Zhu! Time to come out now!"

Mr. Zhu was greatly astonished at this and asked the old priest the reason.

The priest replied, "What explanation can I give?"

This answer was very unsatisfactory to Mr. Zhu; neither did his friend, who was rather frightened, know what to make of it all; so they descended the temple steps and went away.

Finally, with Zhu looking despondent and downcast and Meng in shock and confusion, the two walked slowly down the steps and out of the monastery.

The tale had this to say, "Illusion is born in the mind." These sound like the words of one who has found the Dharma. A man loose in morals will have illusions of lust fulness; when the mind is occupied by lust, it gives rise to a frightful illusion. The Bodhisattva reaches the ignorant that all illusions, however, varied, are the workings of one's own mind. However, despite the earnestness of the old monk's words, the youth failed to gain enlightenment and go off to the mountains, with hair unbound, to seek the Dharma.

TALE 14

The Fox-Fairy Marries Off His Daughter

Minister Yin, now head of the Board of Civil Office, came originally from a poor family in Licheng County, Shandong Province. Though poverty-stricken, young Yin was endowed with considerable physical courage.

In the area where Yin lived, there was a large establishment with an unbroken succession of pavilions and verandahs, which belonged to an old county family. Because ghosts and spirits were frequently seen there, the place had remained occupied and was overgrown with grass and weeds.

One evening when Yin was carousing with some fellow-students, one of them jokingly said, "If anybody will pass a night in the haunted house, the rest of us will stand him a dinner." Yin jumped up at this, and cried out, "What is there difficult in that?" So, taking with him a sleeping-mat, he proceeded thither, escorted by all his companions as far as the door, where they laughed and said, "We will wait here a little while. In case you see anything, shout out to us at once." "If there are any goblins or foxes," replied Yin, "I'll catch them for you."

He then went in, and found the paths obliterated by long grass, which had sprung up, mingled with weeds of various kinds. It was just the time of the new moon, and by its feeble light he was able to make out the door of the house. Feeling his way, he walked on until he reached the back pavilion, and then went up on to the Moon Terrace, which was such a pleasant spot that he determined to stop there. Gazing westwards, he sat for a long time looking at the moon - a, single thread of light embracing in its horns the peak of a hill - without hearing anything at all unusual; so, laughing to himself at the nonsense people talked, he spread his mat upon the floor, put a stone under his head for a pillow, and lay down to sleep.

He had watched the Cow-herd and the Lady until they were just disappearing, and was on the point of dropping off, when suddenly he heard footsteps down below coming up the stairs. Pretending to be asleep, he saw a servant enter, carrying in his hand a lotus-shaped lantern,4 who, on observing Yin, rushed back in a fright, and said to someone behind, "There is a stranger here!"

The person spoken to ask who it was, but the servant did not know; and then up came an old gentleman, who, after examining Yin closely, said, "It's the future President, he's as drunk as can be. We needn't mind him; besides, he's a good fellow, and won't give us any trouble." So they walked in and opened all the doors; and by-and-by there were a great many other people moving about, and quantities of lamps were lighted, till the place was as light as day.

About this time Yin slightly changed his position, and sneezed; upon which the old man, perceiving that he was awake, came forward and fell down on his knees, saying, "I have a daughter who is to be married this very night. It was not anticipated that Your Honour would be here. I pray, therefore, that we may be excused." Yin got up and raised the old man, regret Ding that, in his ignorance of the festive occasion, he had brought with him no present.5 "Sir," replied the old man, "your very presence here will ward off all noxious influences; and that is quite enough for us." He then begged Yin to assist in doing the honors, and thus double the obligation already conferred.

Yin was here to meat a lady, about forty years of age, The old gentleman introduced her as his wife. Someone came saying, "He has come!"

In no long time, a bevy of people with gauze lanterns ushered in the bridegroom himself, who seemed, to be about seventeen or eighteen years old, and of a most refined and prepossessing appearance. The old gentleman bade him pay his respects first to their worthy guest; and upon his looking towards Yin, that gentleman came forward to welcome him on behalf of the host. Then followed ceremonies between the old man and his son-in-law; and when these were over, they all sat down to supper.

Waiting-maids brought in wine and meats, with bowls and cups of jade or gold. When the wine had gone round several times, her father told her to make the proper salutation, after which she went and sat by her mother. Yin saw that she wore on her head beautiful ornaments made of kingfisher's feathers, her beauty quite surpassing anything he had ever seen. He pretended to be tipsy, and leaned forward with his head upon the table as if going off to sleep.

When they were all gone, someone mentioned the sleeping guest, and Yin then arose. It was dark, and he had no light; but he could detect the lingering smell of the food, and the place was filled with the fumes of wine.

Arriving at the door, he found his friends already there; for they had been afraid he might come out after they left, and go in again early in the morning. When he produced the goblet they were all lost in astonishment; and on hearing his story, they were fain to believe it, well knowing that a poor student like Yin was not likely to have such a valuable piece of plate in his possession.

Later on Yin was appointed magistrate over the district of Feiqiu, where there was an old-established family of the name of Zhu. Yin was invited to drink. He now found that these goblets were of precisely the same shape and pattern as the one he had at home, and at once begged his host to tell him where he had had these made. "Well," said Zhu, "there should be eight of them. An ancestor of mine had them made, when he was a minister at the capital, by an experienced artificer. They have been handed down in our family from generation to generation, and have now been carefully laid by for some time; but I thought we would have them out today as a compliment to your Honour. However, there are only seven to be found. None of the servants can have touched them, for the old seals of ten years ago are still upon the box, unbroken. I don't know what to make of it." Yin laughed, and said, "It must have flown away!"

The banquet was over, and Yin went back home. He found the golden cups and ordered someone to take it to that family on horseback. The host took a good look at the cup and was quite amazed. He went to the magistrate's residence and asked where Yin had gotten it. Thereupon, Yin told him the whole story. Now they knew that a fox-fairy was capable of obtaining something from thousands of miles away, but dared not keep it forever.

TALE 15
Witchcraft

When Master Yu was a spirited young fellow, he was fond of boxing and was able to take two kettles and swing them round about with the speed of the wind. Now, during the reign of Chongzhen toward the end of the Ming Dynasty (1368-1644), he went to the capital for the highest imperial examination. While he was here, his servant became seriously ill. Much troubled at this, he applied to a necromancer in the market-place who was skilful at determining the various leases of life allotted to men.

Yu begged him to cast his nativity, which he proceeded to do, finally saying to Yu, "You have but three days to live!"

Yu reflected that Life and Death are already fixed, and he didn't see how magic could save him. So he refused, and was just going away, whereupon the necromancer said, "You grudge this trifling outlay. I hope you will not repent it."

Yu's friends also urged him to pay the money, advising him rather to empty his purse than not secure the necromancer's compassion. Yu, however, would not hear of it, and the three days slipped quickly away. Then he sat down calmly in his inn to see what was going to happen. Nothing did happen all day, and at night he shut his door and trimmed the lamp; then, with a sword at his side, he awaited the approach of death.

Two hours had already gone without bringing him any nearer to dissolution; and he was thinking about lying down, when he heard a scratching at the window, and then saw a tiny little man creep through, carrying a spear on his shoulder, who, on reaching the ground, shot up to the ordinary height. Yu seized his sword and at once struck at it; but only succeeded in cutting the air. His visitor instantly shrank down small again, and made an attempt to escape through the crevice of the window; but Yu redoubled his blows and at last brought him to the ground. Lighting the lamp, he found only a paper man, cut right through the middle. Obviously there came a devil.

Yu prepared to strike, the devil let off an arrow which Yu avoided by jumping aside, the arrow quivering in the wall beyond with a smart crack.

The devil here got very angry, and drawing his sword flourished it like a whirlwind, aiming a tremendous blow, at Yu. Yu ducked, and the whole force of the blow fell upon the stone wall of the house, cutting it right in two.

The devil now became furious, and roared like thunder, turning round to get another blow at his assailant. But Yu again ran between his legs, the devil's sword merely cutting off a piece of his coat.

Yu cut at him right and left, each blow resounding like the watchman's wooden gong, 6 and then, bringing a light, he found it was a wooden image about as tall as a man. The bow and arrows were still there, the latter attached to its waist. Its carved and painted features were most hideous to behold; and wherever Yu had struck it with his sword, there was blood.

The next day, after having told the story far and wide, he went with some others to the place where the necromancer had his stall; but the latter, seeing them coming, vanished in the twinkling of an eye. Someone observed that the blood of a dog would reveal a person who had made himself invisible, and Yu immediately procured some and went back with it. The necromancer disappeared as before, but on the spot where he had been standing they quickly threw down the dog's blood. Thereupon they saw his head and face all smeared over with blood, his eyes glaring like a devil's; and at once seizing him, they handed him over to the authorities, by whom he was put to death.

TALE 16

Buddhist Priest of Changqing

At Changqing there lived a Buddhist priest, who was over eighty years of age. One day he fell down and could not move. When the other priests rushed to help him up, he was found he was already gone.

The old priest's soul flew away to the borders of the province of Hunan. He asked the bystanders for a little hot water, and one among them who loved a joke fetched him some boiling water from a neighboring shop. The priest poured this over the place where he had made the hole, and every eye was fixed upon him when sprouts were seen shooting up, and gradually growing larger and larger.

By-and-by, there was a tree with branches sparsely covered with leaves; then flowers, and last of all fine, large, sweet-smelling pears hanging in great profusion. These the priest picked and handed round to the assembled crowd until all were gone, when he took his pick and hacked away for a long time at the tree, finally cutting it down. This he shouldered, leaves and all, and sauntered quietly away.

Now, from the very beginning, our friend the countryman had been amongst the crowd, straining his neck to see what was going on, and forgetting all about his business. At the departure of the priest he turned round and discovered that every one of his pears was gone. He then knew that those the old fellow had been giving away so freely were really his own pears. Looking more closely at the barrow, he also found that one of the handles was missing, evidently having been newly cut off.

Boiling with rage, he set out in pursuit of the priest, and just as he turned the corner he saw the lost barrow-handle lying under the wall, being in fact the very pear-tree the priest had cut down. But there were no traces of the priest—much to the amusement of the crowd in the market-place.

TALE 17

Jiaona

Scholar Kong Xueli was a descendant of the sage, Confucius. He was a man of forbearance and well-versed in poetry. His good friend, a magistrate of Tiantai County in Zhejiang Province, wrote to invite him to be his guest. He went, only to find on arrival that the magistrate had just passed away. At this point of time, he found himself without the means of returning home; so he took up his abode in a Buddhist monastery, where he was employed in transcribing for the priests.

Not far from this monastery was a house owned by a gentleman named Shan. Shan was wealthy, but he had spent all his money in a heavy law-suit; and this forced him to move his family to a country house, leaving his house vacant.

One snowy day, Kong found it dull, and went out. As he was passing by the door of the above-mentioned house, a young man of very elegant appearance came forth, who, the moment he saw Kong, ran up to him, and asked him to walk in.

Kong followed him inside. The rooms were small, but adorned with embroidered curtains, and scrolls and drawings by celebrated masters. On the table lay a book titled Jottings from Paradise.

Kong asked him why the house had been shut up for so long; to which the young man replied, "This is the Shan family mansion. It has been closed all this time because of the owner's removal into the country. My surname is Huangfu, and my home is in Shensi; but as our house has been burnt down in a great fire, we have put up here for a while."

That evening they spent in laughing and talking together. In the morning, Kong was sitting up with the bed-clothes still huddled round him, when the lad looked in and said, "Master's coming!" Kong jumped up with a start, and in came an old man, who said, "I am very much obliged to you for your condescension in becoming my son's tutor."

The old man presented Kong with an embroidered suit of clothes, a hat, and a Bair of Shoes, plus stockings. After breakfast, the young man handed in his homework written in an archaic style, and not at all after the modern fashion of essay-writing. When Kong asked him why he had done this, the young man replied that he did not contemplate competing at the public examinations.

Next morning, the young man could remember what he had once read, and at the end of two or three months had made astonishing progress. Then they agreed that every five days they would indulge in a symposium, and Miss Perfume should always be of the party.

One night when the wine had gone into Kong's head, he seemed to be lost in a reverie. The young man knew what the matter with him was, saying, "This girl was brought up by my father. I know you find it lonely, and I have long been looking out for a nice wife for you."

One day Kong intended to go out for a stroll in the country, but the young man told him that his father wished to receive no guests for fear of causing interruption to his studies. So Kong thought no more about it; and, when the heat of summer came on, they moved their study to a pavilion in the garden. At this time, Kong had a swelling on the chest about as big as a peach, which, in a single night, increased to the size of a bowl. There he lay groaning with the Bain, while his pupil waited upon him day and night. He slept badly and took hardly any food; and in a few days the place got so much worse that he could neither eat nor drink. The old gentleman also came in, and he and his son lamented over him together.

Then the young man said, "I was thinking last night that my sister, Jiaono, would be able to cure Kong, and accordingly I sent over to my grandmother's asking her to come. She ought to be here by now."

When the girl came, her father and brother ran out to meet her. She was over thirteen years old, and had beautiful eyes. Miss Jiaono immediately rolled up her long sleeves and approached the bed to feel his pulse. As she was grasping his wrist, Kong became conscious of a perfume more delicate than that of the epidendrum.

With one hand she opened her robe and took out a knife with an edge as keen as paper, and pressing the bracelet down all the time with the other, proceeded to cut lightly round near the root of the swelling. The dark blood gushed forth, and stained the bed and the mat; but Kong was delighted to be near such a beauty, not only felt no Bain, but would willingly have continued the operation that she might sit by him a little longer. In a few moments the whole thing was removed, and looked like a growth which had been cut off a tree.

The young lady then said, "He is cured," hurrying away as fast as she could. Her beauty, however, had made such an impression on him that his troubles were hardly at an end. From this moment he gave up his books, and took no interest in anything. This state of things was soon noticed by the young man, who said to him, "My brother, my father has a very high opinion of your talents and would gladly receive you into the family. If you doubt my word, you can wait in the verandah until she takes her daily walk in the garden, and thus Judge for yourself."

Kong saw Miss Jiaono!

A portion of the house was given up to the bride and bridegroom, and the marriage was celebrated with plenty of music and hosts of guests, more like a fairy wedding than anything else.

Kong passed imperial examination, and was given an official position in a county.

One day he went out hunting, and met a handsome young man riding on a nice horse. It was young Huangfu!

One day, young Huangfu seemed troubled in spirit, and said to Kong, "A great calamity is impending. Can you help us?"

Kong did not know what he was alluding to, but readily promised his assistance. The young man then ran out and summoned the whole family to worship in the ancestral hall, at which Kong was alarmed, and asked what it all meant.

"You know," answered

the young man, "I am not a man but a fox. Today we shall be attacked by thunder; and if only you will aid us in our trouble, we may still hope to escape. If you are unwilling, take your child and go, that you may not be involved with us."

Kong promised to be in the same boat with them. The young man placed him with a sword at the door, bidding him remain quiet there in spite of all the thunder. He did as he was told, and saw black clouds obscuring the light until it was all as dark as pitch.

Looking round, he could see that the house had disappeared, and that its place was occupied by a huge mound and a bottomless pit.

Immediately a sharp peal of thunder laid Kong dead upon the ground.

The clouds cleared away, and Jiaono found Kong dead at her feet. She burst out crying at the sight, and declared that she would not live since Kong had died for her.

Jiaono put a red pill into Kong's mouth, and bending down breathed into him. The pill went along with the current of air, and presently there was a gurgle in his throat, and he came round.

TALE 18
Third Sister Hu

Scholar Shang, a native of Taishan, had his living quarters in a small, quiet studio. One autumn night when the Milky Way was unusually clear and the moon shining brightly in the sky, he paced up and down in the garden and his thoughts ran wild.

Suddenly, a young woman came toward him from the other side of the wall and said hello to him. She then told him her name was Hu, and she was called Third Sister.

He was so smitten that he could hardly take his eyes off her, and at last she said to him, "What are you looking at?"

Next night, Third Sister brought her sister, Fourth Sister, a pretty woman with a face delicately powdered. Shang was charmed with her, and inviting them in, began to laugh and talk with the elder, while Third Sister sat playing with her girdle, with her eyes fixed on the ground. Later, Third Sister said she was leaving, whereupon her sister rose to take leave also. Shang asked Fourth Sister not to be in a hurry.

The Fourth Sister stayed put and they chatted without reserve. Finally, Fourth Sister told Shang she was a fox spirit. However, Shang was so occupied with her beauty that he didn't pay any heed to that. Fourth Sister also said, "My sister is very dangerous; she has already killed three people. Anyone bewitched by her has no chance of escape. Happily, you have bestowed your affections on me, and I shall not allow you to be destroyed. You must break off your acquaintance with her at once."

Shang was very frightened, and asked her for help. Fourth Sister replied, "I am a fox, but I am skilled in the arts of the Immortals. I will write out a charm for you which you must paste on the door, and thus you will keep her away."

When her sister came and saw it, Third Sister fell back, crying out, "You've thrown me up for him, have you?"

A few days afterwards Third Sister said she too would have to be absent for a day, so Shang went out for a walk by himself, and suddenly beheld a very nice-looking young lady emerge from the shade of an old oak.

The girl presented Shang with some money, and bade him go on ahead and buy some good wine, adding, "I'll bring something to eat with me, and we'll have a jolly time of it."

Shang took the money and went home, doing as the young lady had told him. Before long, the young lady came, and they now enjoyed themselves.

Third Sister and Fourth Sister came back, and the young lady didn't know where to hide. The two sisters began to revile her, saying, "Out upon you, base fox; what are you doing here?" They then chased her away after some trouble, and Shang began to excuse himself to them, until at last they all became friends again as before.

One day, however, a gentleman came on the back of a donkey. Shang's father asked him where he had come. "I have travelled many miles without being able to find the fox spirits who are now in your house."

Shang and the young ladies had kept their acquaintanceship very dark; but his father and mother invited the gentleman to walk in and perform his exorcisms.

The gentleman produced two bottles which he placed upon the ground, and proceeded to mutter a number of charms and cabalistic formulae, Smoke came out of the bottles.

Shang approached the bottles unperceived, bent his ear to listen. "Ungrateful man," said Third Sister from within, "to sit there and make no effort to save me." This was more than Shang could stand, and he immediately broke the seal, but found that he couldn't untie the knot. "Not so," cried Third Sister. "Lay down the flag that now stands on the altar, and with a pin prick the bladder, and I can get out."

Shang did as she bade him, and in a moment Third Sister jumped out of the bottle.

Years later, Shang was one day superintending his reapers cutting the corn, when he saw Third Sister at a distance, sitting under a tree. He approached, and she took his hand, saying, "Ten years have rolled away since last we met. I missed you very much, so I came to see you once more."

Shang wished her to return home with him, but she refused. As she said this, she disappeared but twenty years later, when Shang was one day alone, Third Sister walked in. Shang was overjoyed, and began to address her; but she said, "My name is already enrolled in the register of the Immortals, and I have no right to return to earth. However, out of my gratitude for you."

TALE 19

A Taoist Priest

Mr. Han from a wealthy family was fond of entertaining people. A man named Xu, of the same town, frequently joined him over the food.

On one occasion when they were together, a Taoist priest came to the door with his alms-bowl in his hand. Mr. Han invited him to come in and be seated. However, Mr. Xu treated him all the time with a certain amount of disrespect because of his shabby appearance.

When the priest had drunk over twenty large cups of wine, he intended to take his leave.

Xu said to him in raillery, "You seem to be like a guest!"

Replied the priest, "I am much the same as yourself - a bag for food from Han!"

Xu felt shamed, and had no answer to make.

When they had finished drinking, the priest proposed to have the pleasure of their company the following day at noon. Han and Xu went and found the priest was waiting for them in the street. The three passed through a handsome courtyard, and the three went inside, and found it was magnificently decorated.

They instantly felt more respect for their host; and no sooner had they sat down than wine and food were served by well dressed boys, all about sixteen years of age.

They began dining and wining. The priest cried out, "Call the Shi sisters!"

In a few minutes, two elegant young ladies walked in. One was tall and slim and the other short and very young, both being exceedingly pretty girls. They sang for them. The singing was followed by dancing. When the dance concluded, the girls leant against a painted screen, and the two guests were at last irrecoverably drunk.

In the next day morning, Han and Xu woke up but they found themselves lying in the road, with Mr. Xu's head in a dirty drain.

TALE 20

Stone from the Heaven

A man named Cheng was a friend of a man named Chou. Cheng was poor and depended very much on Chou, and he called Chou's wife "sister". Unfortunately, this wife happened to die in child-bed, and Chou married another named Wang. Wang was a young girl, and Cheng did not seek to be introduced.

One day Wang's younger brother came, and was entertained in the inner house, when Cheng chanced to call. Chou asked him in, but Cheng would not enter. Chou ordered the servant to move the family feast to the public part of the house, and Cheng came and joined them.

Someone came saying a former servant had been severely beaten at the magistrate's Yamen. In the next day morning, he said to his family, "The magistrate should not be the servant of influential people. If there is a case of any kind, he should hear both plaintiff and defendant."

When Cheng was told Chou had gone into the city, he immediately hurried after him, but Chou was already in the jail. Cheng managed to gain admittance to the jail. When the two met,

Cheng proposed that a petition should be presented direct to the imperial court.

The emperor received Cheng's petition. It was then more than ten months since the beginning of the affair, and Chou, who was already under sentence of death. The officers of the Board of Punishments were very much alarmed when they received the emperor's instructions, and set to work to re-hear the case in person.

At that point of time, the jailers were bribed to kill Chou. Fortunately, the Board officer investigated the case himself, and found that Chou was in the last stage of starvation. Jailers were bambooed to death. The magistrate was banished for perversion of the law, and Chou was permitted to return home.

When Chou was in jail, Cheng took a dismal view of human affairs. Now Chou had been set free, he asked Chou to retire with him from the world. However, Chou was deeply attached to his young wife, so he threw cold water on the proposition. Cheng pursued the subject no farther and was nowhere to be found after that.

Eight years had passed away, when suddenly Cheng re-appeared, clad in a yellow cap and wearing a Taoist robe. Chou was delighted. Chou then ordered wine, and they chatted together on what had taken place in the interval. He also tried to persuade Cheng to detach himself from the Taoist persuasion, but Cheng only smiled and answered nothing. Chou asked where he lived, and Cheng replied, "In the Great Pure Mansion on Mount Lao."

They then retired to sleep on the same bed. That night, Chou dreamed that Cheng was lying on his chest so that he could not breathe. In a fright he asked him what he was doing, but got no answer; and then he waked up with a start. Calling to Cheng and receiving no reply, he sat up and stretched out his hand to touch him. However, Cheng had vanished. When he got calm, he found he was lying at Cheng's end of the bed, which rather startled him.

He seized a mirror to look at himself, and found in the mirror it is Cheng.

"If this is Cheng, where on earth am I?" By this time he was wide awake, and knew that Cheng had employed magic to induce him to retire from the world. He was on the point of entering the ladies' apartments; but his brother, not recognizing who he was, stopped him, and would not let him go in. As he himself was unable to prove his own identity, he ordered his horse that he might go in search of Cheng.

When he arrived at Mount Lao; he saw a great number of Taoist priests and among them was one who stared fixedly at him. He asked a priest where he should find Cheng. The priest laughed and said, "I know the name. He is probably in the Great Pure Mansion."

Finally, Chou found Cheng, who invited his friend to sit down with him. At dawn, he was anxious to return home, but Cheng pressed him to stay; and when three days had gone by Cheng said to him, "Tomorrow I will set you on your way."

When Chou returned home he found his wife was killed by gangsters. As he was an unpractical man, his wealth was gone and the family reduced to poverty. Chou's son, who was growing up, was thus unable to secure the services of a tutor, and had no one but his uncle to teach him.

One morning, on going into the school-room, the uncle found a letter lying on his desk addressed to himself in his brother's handwriting. In it was a finger-nail about four inches in length. He laid the nail down on the ink-slab and found that the ink-stone changed into a piece of shining yellow gold. Then he tried the nail on copper and iron things, all of them were likewise turned to gold. He thus became very rich, and shared his wealth with Cheng's son.

TALE 21
The Repentant Tiger

Once upon a time there was an old lady in her seventies who had only one son. One day, her son went into the mountains and was eaten by a tiger. The old lady was so grieved that she nearly committed suicide. When she went to see the county magistrate and wept in front of him, the official laughed, "It a tiger that killed your son. How do you expect me to use my power to punish a wild beast?" The old lady howled when she heard these words. The county magistrate criticized her, but she was not afraid. Taking her age into consideration, the county magistrate could not bring himself to be unsympathetic, so he promised her that he would try to have the tiger caught and take revenge for her loss. She knelt on the ground and would not get up until the document was issued ordering the capture of the tiger. So the county magistrate asked of his staff who would volunteer to catch the tiger. One man, by the name of Li Neng, who happened to be drunk at the moment, walked up to the official and took the job. Only then did the old lady get up and leave the county government office.

As soon as he awoke from the stupor, Li Neng regretted his foolishness. Still he believed that the order issued by the county magistrate to catch the tiger was only a show and a method to free the magistrate from the nagging of the old lady. As a result, Li did not really carry out the order, but took the document back with him to the government office. The county magistrate was enraged, saying, "Since you've promised to do it, there is no way for you to be allowed to take back your word!" Embarrassed, Li Neng finally asked to have all the hunters in the county gathered. Then he took them to the mountain valley in the hope of catching a tiger and reporting that the job was done.

Over a month passed and Li Neng was punished with several hundred lashings for failing the job. Having no other place to pour out his grievances, Li went to pray at the Mountain God Temple in the eastern suburbs. Soon, a tiger came in, catching Li off guard. The tiger, however, prostrated itself in the center of the room. Li prayed, "If you are the one who ate the old lady's son, please lower your head and let me tie you up." So saying, he tied a rope around the tiger's head without meeting with any resistance from the beast.

Li took the tiger to the county government office where the county magistrate questioned the tiger, "Were you the one who ate the old lady's son?" The tiger nodded its head. The magistrate went on, "Paying for a life you've taken with your own life has been a rule since antiquity, besides the man was the old lady's only son. How can she live in such an advance age without the care of her son? If you can serve as her son, I'll let you free." The tiger nodded its head again. The magistrate had it unbound so that the tiger could leave.

Although she complained that the county magistrate had let the tiger go instead of avenging her son, the lady opened her gate in the morning and found a deer, which had already been killed. She sold the deer meat and skin and used that money to support the family. Such things happened pretty often. Sometimes, you could see the tiger bringing in money and silk in its mouth. In a way the tiger was more filial than her son and quietly she felt grateful to the tiger. When the tiger came, it would lie under the eaves all day long. She and the tiger lived in harmony.

Several years later, the old lady died and the tiger roared in the living room. The savings of the old lady were more than enough to cover her funeral. As soon as the tomb was built, the tiger rushed to the sight, frightening away the guests. The tiger went straight to the tomb, roaring even more loudly. It did not leave until it had vented its grief. The locals built the Virtuous Tiger Temple, which still stands today.

TALE 22

The Fight between Mantis and Snake

A certain Mr. Zhang was walking in a mountain valley and heard a loud noise from the cliffs. He climbed up the cliffs and saw a huge snake tossing in the trees, its tail beating willows and breaking willow branches. Its desperate tossing and turning suggested that it was being gripped by something. Mr. Zhang looked closely but found nothing. He became more curious and walked nearer to the snake. This time he saw a mantis clinging to the snake's head, cutting the snake head with its forearms as sharp as swords. Despite whatever the snake did, it could not throw off the mantis. Eventually, the snake died. Skin and flesh had been peeled off from its forehead.

TALE 23

The Barrow Pusher

A man was pushing a wheel barrow uphill. Just then a wolf bit into his back. He wanted to let loose of the barrow so as to fight the wolf, but was afraid the barrow would roll back on him. So he continued pushing the barrow despite the pain in his back. When he reached the hill top, the wolf ran away, having bitten a large chunk of meat from his back.

To bite someone when he is in difficulty is one of the most absurd things to do.

TALE 24
The Scorpion Merchant

A scorpion trader from the south came to Linju, Shandong, every year to purchase a large quantity of scorpions. The local people were kept busy, catching scorpions with wooden clippers, from caves and under stones in the mountains. One year, the scorpion merchant came again and stayed in a hotel. Suddenly he was gripped by pain in his chest. He said to the hotel owner, "I've taken too many lives. I have upset the scorpion spirit. Now he wants to kill me. Please help me to save my life." The hotel owner saw a big vat in the room and so he asked the merchant to squat down and covered him up with the vat. Just then a man with a ferocious look and yellowish hair came in the room, searching and sniffing. Then he walked out. The hotel owner sighed with relief, saying, "It's safe now." He removed the vat only to find nothing but blood.

TALE 25

Wife Turned into a Pig

Du Xiaolei, a native of Xishan, Yidu County, Shandong, was a devoted and kind son to his blind mother. Though the family was poor, they were never without food.

One day before he set out on a trip, Du bought some meat and told his wife to prepare dumplings for his mother. Du's wife was a vicious person. She put some dung-beetles into the minced meat used as filling for the dumplings. When the blind mother tasted the foul dumplings, she decided they were impossible to eat. So she saved them for her son to see.

When he came home, Du greeted his mother and asked, "Did you enjoy the dumplings?" His mother shook her head and showed him the dumplings. Du opened one and found the dung-beetles inside. Enraged, he wanted to beat his wife, but on second thought he was afraid that his mother would hear. Deep in thought, he did not answer when his wife talked to him. His wife was disappointed and paced in front of the bed. Du snorted, "Why don't you go to bed? Are you waiting for some kind of punishment?" When he heard no response from his wife, he got up and lit a candle. There he found a pig that had human feet. He realized that the pig was originally his wife.

After the county magistrate heard this story, he ordered the pig be bound up and shown to the public as a warning to people.

TALE 26
Grateful Wolves

Mao Dafu, a native of Taihang, Shanxi, was a doctor specialized in curing sores. One day on his way back from visiting a patient, he saw a wolf dropping a package from his mouth and then crouching by the roadside. Mao Dafu picked up the bundle and was surprised to find jewelry inside. The wolf jumped out of the bushes and dragged him by his trousers. Mao Dafu struggled to get away, but the wolf continued to pull at his clothes. Realizing the wolf was not trying to hurt him, he decided to follow it into the woods.

They reached a cave in which a sick wolf was lying on the ground. The wolf had a festering sore on his head. The situation was so bad that maggots could be seen crawling on the sore. Mao Dafu understood what the wolf meant. He cut off the rotten flesh and then put some medicine on the sore before he left. The day was already dark. The wolf escorted him down the mountainside. After walking quite a distance, he encountered a pack of wolves that was about to attack him. But the wolf he had been walking with approached the pack and seemed to speak to them. Soon they made way for Mao Dafu, who was able to reach his home safe and sound.

Not long before this, Ning Tai, a silverware dealer in the county, was killed by some robbers. There were no clues in the case. When Mao Dafu was trying to sell the jewelry he received from the wolf, the Ning family members recognized them. They sent Mao Dafu to the court. Mao Dafu told the court how he obtained the jewelry, but the magistrate would not believe him. The bailiffs shackled him and locked him away. Mao Dafu felt that only the wolves could prove his innocence, so the court sent him along with two clerks to the cave in the mountain. Since the wolves did not come back during the daytime, the three returned without seeing the evidence. On their way down from the mountain they met two wolves. One had a scar on his head, and Mao Dafu recognized it. He bowed to the wolf, saying, "Last time you gave me some gifts but now they have caused trouble. I am being accused of stealing them. If you don't help me to prove my innocence, I will be beaten to death." The wolf angrily charged at the two clerks. The clerks took out their swords. As the wolves howled into the night, hundreds of wolves from all over the mountain appeared in the woods, surrounding the clerks. The wolves bit at the rope binding Mao Dafu. The clerks understood the wolves and hurriedly untied the rope. Then the wolves walked away.

The magistrate was intrigued by the tale, but did not immediately release Mao Dafu. Several days later a court official was traveling along a country path. A wolf emerged from the trees and placed a shoe in front of the official. The official ordered his staff to pick up the shoe, and the wolf disappeared into the trees. After he returned to the court, the official secretly sent people to find out who the owner of the shoe was. Someone said that it belonged to a man named Cong Xin, who was once chased by wolves and lost his shoe. The officials asked Cong Xin to tell whether the shoe belonged to him, and investigators eventually discovered it was Cong Xin who had killed the silverware dealer, Ning Tai. After Cong Xin killed the dealer, he bundled a great deal of silver and jewelry in a jacket. Before he had time to take the jewelry away, the wolves attacked him and he ran away, leaving the bundle to the wolves.

Once upon a time, a midwife met a wolf on her way back from a trip. The wolf bit at her clothes, trying to make her follow. The midwife went into the hills and found a bitch in labor. The midwife helped with the delivery. The next day, the wolf left a piece of venison outside the midwife's house as a payment of her kindness. Many similar stories are told among the hill villagers.

TALE 27

Snake Woman

Gao Meng from Feixian County in Shandong Province once described a strange case he came across when he worked as governor of Chengdu.

A businessman from the west settled in Chengdu and married a widow from the Qingcheng Mountains. Later, the businessman returned to the west on business and after a year came once again to Chengdu. When the couple met and slept together that evening, the businessman died suddenly. His partners suspected his wife and reported the case to the court, which also suspected that the businessman's wife might have had a love affair and plotted to kill her husband. They tortured the woman but she professed her innocence. While preparing documents on the case, the court realized there was not enough proof to close the case. They threw the widow into jail and thus the case dragged on without a sound conclusion.

According to Gao Meng, someone in the court fell ill and an old doctor of traditional medicine was brought to the court to treat him. In one of their conversations, the case was mentioned.

Hearing about the case, the old doctor asked whether the widow's mouth was rather pointed. The court officials asked him if that had anything to do with the case. It took the doctor some time to make up his mind and finally he said, "Many ladies in several villages in the Qingcheng Mountains made love with snakes. Then they had babies with pointed mouths. They also had something like a snake tongue in their vagina. When they grew up and made love with men, the tongue-like thing would slither into the penis, killing the man instantly."

Gao Meng was very surprised to hear this and found it hard to believe. The old doctor said, "A witch living nearby has some medicine that will help arouse a woman's sexual desire which will make the tongue-like thing appear. Whether what I've said is true can be easily tested." Gao Meng forced the widow to swallow the medicine and then observed her sexual organs. Sure enough, something shaped like the tongue of a snake appeared. The lady who was suspected of deliberately killing her husband was thus proven innocent. The legal documents concerning the case were handed over to the provincial authorities, who also used the same method to verify the woman's innocence. All charges against her were dismissed.

TALE 28

Bird Envoys

A man called Shi Wucheng in Yuancheng near Nanjing had no job and stayed at home all day long. A flock of birds gathered on the roof of his house. They looked and sounded like crows. Shi Wucheng said to his family members, "My wife has sent bird envoys to take me away. Please prepare for my funeral. I'm going to die soon."

On that very day, he died. During the funeral, the flock of crows came again, hovering over the coffin all the way from Yuancheng to Xingting. They disappeared after the man was buried.

Wu Muxin from Changshan, Shandong, witnessed what had happened.

TALE 29
Judge Lu

One day, when Zhu Ertan in Lingyang dined together with his friends, one of them said jokingly, "If you have the guts to go at night to the Chamber of Horrors, and bring back the Infernal Judge from the left-hand porch, we'll stand you a dinner."

Zhu smiled, and went straight off to the temple; and before long his friends heard him shouting, "His Excellency has arrived!" And in came Zhu with the image on his back, which he proceeded to deposit on the table, and then

poured out a triple libation in its honour. His friends felt ill at ease, and begged him to carry the Judge back to the temple again.

Zhu carried the Judge back, and the next day his friends gave him the promised dinner, from which he went home half-tipsy in the evening.

Not feeling he had had enough wine, he helped himself to another cup. Suddenly, the Judge came and said to Zhu, "It is warm today, shall we drink the wine cold?"

"My name is Lu," replied the Judge. "I have no other names." They began to drink out of each other's cups. When Zhu got tipsy and went to bed first, the Judge drank by himself. In his drunken sleep Zhu felt a Bain in his stomach, and woke up to find the Judge had opened him and was carefully arranging his inside.

Zhu observed the Judge place a piece of flesh upon the table, and asked him what it was. "Your heart," said the Judge. "Don't be afraid. I am just installing a more intelligent heart inside your body."

Zhu studied very hard but he was not successful in his career. After this "surgical operation", however, Zhu successfully passed the imperial examination.

TALE 30

The Magic Sword

Ning Caichen in Zhejiang was a good-natured man. One day, when he paid visit to a temple to the north of the city where he lived, he found with great surprise that the doors of the rooms there were ajar, with the exception of a small room on the south side, where the lock had a new appearance.

There he met a man who told Ning his name was Yin Chixia, and he lived there. At night, as he was dropping off to sleep, he perceived that somebody was in the room. Jumping up in great haste, he found it was a young lady who was going to attempt to bewitch him. He sternly bade her begone.

Next day, a young candidate for the examination came and lodged in the east room with his servant. However, he was killed that very night, and his servant the night after. Their corpses showed a small hole in the sole of the foot. When Yin was asked what he thought about it, he said that it was the work of devils.

In the middle of the night a lady appeared and said to him, "I, Xiao Qian. I died at eighteen and was buried in this temple. A devil forced me to bewitch people by my beauty."

By the time when she was to leave, she wept, and said, "I am about to sink into the sea. But your sense of duty is boundless. If you will collect my bones and bury them in some quiet spot, I shall not again be subject to these misfortunes."

Ning said he would do so, and she told him where she was buried, "At the foot of the aspen-tree on which there is a bird's nest."

At night, Ning pretended to be asleep in order to watch what happened. His roommate Yin opened a box, and took out something which he smelt and examined by the light of the moon. He then wrapped it up carefully and put it back in the broken box, "I am a Taoist priest. I have already killed the devil."

Next day he found traces of blood outside the window which led round to the north of the temple; and there among a number of graves he discovered the aspen tree with the bird's nest at its summit. He then fulfilled his promise and prepared to go home, Yin giving him a farewell banquet, and presenting him with an old leather case which he said contained a sword, and would keep at a distance from him all devils and bogies.

Ning then said to Yin that he had a younger sister buried in the temple, so he and Yin dug up Xiao Qian's bones, and hired a boat to bring them to an area, where he made a grave and buried the bones there. After this, he was proceeded home when he suddenly heard himself addressed from behind, "Let me go home with you and wait upon your father and mother; you will not repent it." Looking closely at her, he observed that she had a beautiful complexion.

They went back home together. Now Ning's wife had been in for a long time, and his mother advised him not to say a word about it to her for fear of frightening her. Xiao Qian asked permission to see Ning's wife, but this was denied. Xiao Qian then went into the kitchen and got ready the dinner, running about the place as if she had lived there all her life.

Ning's mother was much afraid of Xiao Qian, and would not let her sleep in the house; so Xiao Qian went to live in the study. When she was just entering there, she suddenly fell back a few steps, and began walking hurriedly backwards and forwards in front of the door.

Ning called out and asked her what it meant, and she replied, "The presence of that sword frightens me." Ning at once hung up the sword-case in another place. She asked Ning if he studied at night or not. Ning said he would, and they sat silently there for some time, after which Xiao Qian went away and took up her quarters elsewhere.

For many days, Xiao served Ning's mother very well during the day. She, as a devil, had not tasted meat since her arrival. Towards the end of six months, she began to take a little thin gruel. Mother and son alike became very fond of her.

One day Xiao Qian said, "I fear that the devil at the temple is angry at my escape, and may come suddenly and carry me off."

At night Xiao Qian warned Ning not to go to sleep; but nothing more was heard, and the sword-case resumed its original size. Ning was greatly alarmed, but Xiao Qian said, "There's an end to my troubles."

After these events Ning passed the imperial examination and Xiao Qian bore him a son.

TALE   31

A Considerate Husband

When a man surnamed Zhu died at the age of fifty, his family members heard him cry out in the coffin. They rushed over and found he had come to life again.

Zhu told his family he came to life because he missed his wife very much.

"I would die directly later so long as I had enough from her," he said.

"Well, how can you die again directly?" asked his wife curiously.

Zhu said, "Just go and make preparation for me."

The old lady laughed and Zhu urged her to do according to what he had said.

The wife went inside the house to make bed for her husband, and the two lay down to enjoy themselves.

The old lady was happy to be with her husband. Before long, however, she ceased smiling, and her two eyes closed.

For a long time not a sound was heard, as if she was fast asleep. When the other family members came in, they found she was dead, and her husband had passed away too.

TALE 32

A Magnanimous Girl

A young man surnamed Ku in the Qinling area was pov-erty-stricken. As he had an old mother to take care of, he hated to leave home. So he made a living by doing writing or painting for others.

By the time when he was twenty-five years old, he was still not married. His next door neighbor was occupied by an old lady and a girl. When Ku's mother went to visit, she found the girl's mother was deaf, and they were poverty-stricken too. Mrs. Ku returned home and told her son, saying, "The girl doesn't speak or laugh, but she is very nice-looking."

One day, as Ku was doing his reading in his study, an agree-able young fellow came. He said he was from a neighboring vil-lage, and hoped Ku would draw a picture for him. The two youths soon struck up a firm friendship and met constantly, when it hap-pened that the young man chanced to see the young lady.

"Who is that?" he asked, following her with his eyes. Ku told him she was his next door neighbor. The young man said, "She is just pretty, but rather stern in her appearance."

"She's a good daughter," said Ku's mother. "We need to do our best to help her and her mother."

One day, Ku's mother found she got an abscess on her leg. The young lady soothed her and gave her medicine. As she was with Ku's mother, Ku walked in.

Ku's mother said to her son, "I am deeply indebted to her. Please do not forget to repay her kindness."

One day, Ku managed to squeeze her hand, but she told him never to do so again.

She disliked to see Ku talk with the young man mentioned above. Once when he came, she got angry at something he said, and drew from her robe a glittering knife about a foot long. The young man ran out in a fright. She then threw her dagger up into the air…

On the ground was a dead white fox.

"He's your friend," cried the girl.

Next day the young lady came, and told Ku to keep it secret or it might be prejudicial to his happiness. She then took her leave.

TALE 33

Fox Friend

Che was a young man who was not particularly well off. He was so fond of drinking that he would be unable to sleep at night.

One night he fancied one was in the bed with him, but he instantly realized it was only the clothes which had slipped off. He stretched out his hand to feel, and found it was a fox sleeping like a dog. In order not to startle the animal, he slept with his arm across it.

In small hours, the fox woke up and transformed himself into a young man, and Che said, "Well, you've had a nice sleep!"

As it was still too early to get up, they went to sleep again. Che urged the young man to visit him, and the fox agreed. Next day morning, when Che awoke, he found his fox friend had already disappeared.

Next evening, the fox man arrived, and said to Che, "Two miles away, you will find some silver lying by the wayside. Go early in the morning and get it."

Che set off early in the morning, and did obtain two silver ingots, with which he later bought some food and wine. Che cried, "I shall have no more anxiety about funds for buying wine with all this in my purse."

"Well," said the fox man, "I must do something further for you."

Days later, the fox man said to Che, "Buckwheat is very cheap in the market. It is a chance to make money now."

Che bought over forty tons of buckkwheat, and many said he was a fool. Before long, however, there was a bad drought and all kinds of grain and beans were spoilt. Only buckwheat would grow, and Che sold off his stock and made lots of money.

The fox treated Che's wife as his own sister, and Che's children as his own. When Che died of old age, he never came to the house again.

TALE 34

Miss Lin Xiang

Sang Ziming, a young man in Yizhou, was an orphan when quite young. He went out of home only twice a day for his meals to a neighbor's close by. For most of the time, he sat quietly at home.

One day, a young lady knocked at his door, and Sang opened it and asked her to walk in. She said her name was Lin Xiang, and lived not very far off. After that, Lin Xiang dropped in frequently for a chat; but one evening when Sang was sitting alone expecting her, another young lady suddenly came. She was about fifteen or sixteen years of age, wore very full sleeves, and dressed her hair after the fashion of unmarried girl.

Sang took her for a fox, but the girl said, "My name is Li, and I am of a respectable family. Hearing of your talent, I hope to be one of your friends."

Sang laughed, and took her by the hand, which he found was as cold as ice. When asked the reason, she told him that she had always been delicate. She then remarked that she intended to visit him pretty frequently, and hoped it would not inconvenience him.

Sang said no one came to see him except another young lady, and that not very often. "When she comes, I'll go," replied the girl.

She then gave him an embroidered slipper, and said that whenever he shook it she would know that he wanted to see her.

One evening after this, Lin Xiang came, and said in alarm to Sang, "Whatever has made you look so melancholy?" Sang replied that he did not know, and she took her leave, saying they would not meet again for some ten days.

During the ten days, Li visited Sang every day. One day, she asked Sang who was better, Lin or her.

"Both of you are perfect," replied Sang. "You are a little colder than her."

The next evening, Lin Xiang came, and suddenly exclaimed, "Oh, dear! How much worse you seem to have become in the last ten days. You must have encountered something bad."

Lin went on to explain, "You look bad and your pulse is very thready. You've got the devil-disease."

The following evening when Li came, Sang asked her what she thought of Lin Xiang.

"Oh, she is just pretty, but she's a fox," Li said. "I followed her to her hole on the hill-side."

Sang attributed what Li said to jealousy, but the next evening when Lin Xiang came, he observed, "Someone has told me you are a fox."

Sang declared at first that it was only a joke of his, but later let out the whole story.

"She is surely not a human being." Lin Xiang said.

The following evening Li came in, and they Lin Xiang entered and said to Sang, "She is a devil, and if you do not at once forbid her coming here, you will soon be on the road to the other world."

Sang did feel bad when he examined himself.

The next evening Lin Xiang boiled some medicine for Sang, which made him feel much better. After some days, he recovered and Lin Xiang left him, warning him to have no more to do with Li.

Next evening, Lin Xiang came and found out that Miss Li had been there again. Lin told Sang he would certainly die if he continued to be with Li.

Two months passed away, and Sang began to experience a feeling of great lassitude. He became very thin, and could only take thick gruel.

He said to Li, "I am sorry I didn't listen to Lin Xiang before I got as bad as this."

He then closed his eyes and kept them shut for some time. When he opened them again, Li had disappeared. Sang lay on his bed to wait for the return of Lin Xiang.

One day, Lin Xiang came. She said, "When the disease has reached at this stage, there is very little to be done. I merely came to say goodbye to you."

Sang asked her to take slipper from under his pillow and destroy it, but Lin turned it over and over. All at once Li walked in, but when she saw Lin Xiang she turned back as though she would run away. Lin Xiang prevented by placing herself in the doorway.

Li bent her head in acknowledgment of her guilt, and Lin Xiang continued, "How is it that a nice girl like you can thus turn love into hate?"

Li begged for mercy. "I am a daughter of a petty official named Li, and I died young."

Lin Xiang said, "How shall we cure him?"

Lin Xiang opened a bag and drew forth some drugs and said, "I have been looking forward to this day. The only condition is that it be administered by the very hand which wrought the ill."

Li put the pills Lin Xiang gave her into Sang's mouth. Lin Xiang cried out, "He is cured!"

Just at this moment Li heard the cock crow and vanished, and Lin Xiang remained. Day and night she took care of him, and every evening Li came in to render assistance.

Three months afterwards Sang was as strong as ever he had been, and then for several evenings Li ceased to visit them, seeming very uneasy in her mind.

TALE   35

The Fighting Quail

Wang Cheng from an old family in Pingyuan used to be wealthy but he squandered everything available except an old house.

Wang had been told of his grandfather's fox-wife. He decided to invite her to return with him and she did.

Wang asked his wife to meet her, but when she came with unkempt hair and dirty face, the old woman shook her head. She looked at the smokeless stove, and said, "How have you managed even to support life?" Wang's wife told her how poor they were and sobbed. The old woman gave her a hair-pin, asked her to go pawn it. With the proceeds thus gained, she could buy some food. She said she would visit them again.

Three days later, she returned, and produced some money. She passed the night with them, and Mrs. Wang was at first rather frightened.

Next day, the old lady said to Wang, "Grandson, you should try to make some money to keep the family going."

Wang told her he had no capital, but the old lady said, "I have forty ounces of silver. Take it."

She also warned him, saying, "Be neither lazy nor slow."

Wang worked hard but didn't make money. He had no way out but to face his grandmother empty-handed, and he remained in a very undecided state, until suddenly he saw a quail-catcher winning heaps of money by Fighting his birds, and selling them at over 100 cash apiece. He then determined to lay out his five ounces of silver in quails.

He bought his quails, but he found some were dead and others dying. He was quite at a loss as to what to do. The next day, a lot more had died, and only a few were left. The day after this he went again to look at them, and found only a single quail survived.

Wang was advised to train his bird and take it into the street and gamble for something to eat. This, too, he did, and his quail won every main. Everything turned out favorably, and by the end of six months he had saved twenty ounces of silver, so that he became quite easy in his mind and looked upon the quail as a dispensation of his destiny.

A local Prince raised quails too, but his quail was signally defeated by Wang's. Finally, he ordered to release his Jade Bird from the palace, and said to Wang, "If your quail is killed I will make it up to you handsomely."

Wang then released his bird, and the Prince's quail rushed at it at once. Before long, the Prince's Jade Bird made its escape. Wang won again. From this he won lots of money.

TALE 36

The Painted Skin

When a man named Wang was taking a stroll in an open area in Taiyuan in a morning, he saw a young lady with a bundle on her back. Wang went over and found she was a pretty girl of about sixteen.

"May I help you?" said Wang.

"My parents sold me to a rich man as his concubine. His wife was very jealous, and beat me every day. This forces me to run away," the girl said.

Wang promised he would keep secret for her. He then told his wife, but his wife feared the girl might invite trouble for them. Still, they allowed the girl to live with them.

One day, Wang met a Taoist priest, who said, "You are bewitched."

When Wang returned home, door to his study was shut, which made him suspect that something was wrong. He climbed over the wall, and found the door of the inner room was shut too. He saw through the window a hideous devil, with a green face and jagged teeth like a saw, spreading a human skin upon the bed, was drawing with a paint brush. The devil then put aside the brush, and threw it over its shoulders, and then turned into the girl living with them in the house.

Wang was frightened and hurried away to look for that priest.

The priest gave Wang a magic note to be hung at the door of the bedroom. Wang did so upon home.

When the devil saw the magic note, she stood looking at it without venturing to get closer.

Wang's wife, who was in an agony of fright, hardly dared cry for fear of making a noise. Wang invited the priest to help, and the priest came with a wooden sword. Standing in the center of the courtyard, he shouted out at the devil. The devil tried to get away, but the priest struck her with his wooden sword. She lay grunting like a pig, until the priest struck off her head and she then became a dense column of smoke curling up from the ground.

TALE 37

Clever Boy

In Hunan there was a man who did business out of the region, leaving behind his wife. She yearned to have someone to be with her at night. One night, the one came but she found it was a small creature - a fox.

Out of her fear of fox spirit, she asked her maid and her ten-year-old son to come and keep her company at night.

Next day night came, and the fox appeared. When the maid called out, the fox ran away. From then on, when night came, the trader's wife dared not blow out the candle.

One day, the boy moved from the door a little way, when suddenly out rushed something like a fox, which was disappearing through the door. He lost no time to cut off about two inches of its tail, from which the warm blood was still dripping. When his mother came out of her room, he pretended not to hear her, regretting only as he went to bed that he hadn't killed the fox.

On the morrow he followed the tracks of blood over the wall and into the garden of a family named Ho. When his father came back home, the boy told him what had happened and the man was much alarmed. He sent for a doctor to attend his wife, but the woman only threw the medicine away, and cursed and swore horribly. They secretly mixed the medicine with her tea and soup, and in a few days she began to get better.

At night, the husband woke up and found his wife gone. He and his won discovered her sleeping in another room. From that time she became more eccentric than ever, and was always being found in strange places, cursing those who tried to remove her.

One evening the boy hid himself in the Ho family garden. As the moon rose he saw two people drinking, dressed in an old dark-brown coat. The boy saw that both of them had tails.

One day, the boy found out the long-bearded man, and bought him some wine to drink.

That night his mother slept well, and the boy knew that something must have happened.

He then told his father, and they went to see if there were any results. They found both foxes stretched out dead! The wine-bottle there was empty.

From that time they were left in peace.

TALE 38

The Laughing Girl

Wang Zufu in Shandong was an orphan but he was a clever boy who passed local examination at the age of fourteen. His mother loved him very much and hated to see he strayed far away from home.

One day his cousin Wu came, and Wang wept bitterly at the sight of his cousin. Wang told him he loved a girl walking in the country, but he had no news about her at all.

Wu said, "I'll make inquiries for you. If she's not already engaged, I have no doubt we can arrange the affair."

What Wu did in the next few days proved fruitless.

Wang shook his head at this, and sat day after day waiting for Wu, until his patience was thoroughly exhausted. He decided to go and find the girl himself.

He found a small house down in the valley, and began to descend the hill and make his way thither. There he heard a girl's voice wafted from the house calling out Xiao Jung.

The girl emerged and, as soon as she raised her face, she saw

Wang, and stopped working.

An old woman, leaning on a stick, asked Wang where he came from and what he came for. Wang told her everything, and the old lady laughed and said, "It is a funny thing to look for a girl when you don't know her. Come in and have something to eat."

After Wang had had enough food, the old woman said, "Call Miss Ning."

After some time there was a giggling at the door, and the old woman cried out, "Ying Ning! Your cousin is here."

There was then a great tittering as a maid pushed her in. Wang made her a bow, and the old woman said, "Wang is your cousin; you have never seen him before. Isn't that funny?"

Wang asked how old his cousin was, and the old woman said, "She is sixteen, and as foolish as a baby."

"One year younger than I am," said Wang.

Next day morning, Wang came across Ying Ning in the back yard. Ying Ning asked him why he came here, Wang told her he could not forget her since he met her that day.

When Wang told her husband and wife were always together, Ying Ning said it was something she did not like.

Wang was angry with her for being so dull, but there was no help for it. Finally, Ying Ning agreed to go with him to see her aunt. Wang and Ying Ning then took their leave.

When they met Wu, Wu asked, "Is this young lady's name Ying Ning? A fox had a daughter named Ying Ning. The fox then went away, taking Ying Ning with it, and now here she is."

Wu said he would go and find out for them all about Ying Ning and her queer story, so as to be able to arrange the marriage.

Wang's mother set an auspicious day for the wedding, but still feeling suspicious about Ying Ning.

One evening Ying Ning went in tears to her husband, and

said, "I am the daughter of a fox. When my mother went away she put me in the charge of the disembodied spirit of an old woman. Now my foster-mother is lying on the hill-side with no one to bury her and appease her discontented shade. If not too much, I would ask you to do this, that her spirit may be at rest, and know that it was not neglected by her whom she brought up."

Wang agreed and did according to what Ying Ning had told him.

TALE 39
Young Zhu

Li Hua in Changzhou had an only daughter named Xiao-hui, but she died of a severe illness at fourteen. Li Hua was fifty years of age and bought a concubine, who bore him a son, called Zhu, or the Pearl. When the boy was five years old, he could hardly talk plainly. His father, however, loved him very much, and did not observe his faults.

One day, a one-eye priest came to collect alms, and he declared he had control over life, death, happiness, and misfortune. When Li went over to him, he demanded one hundred of ounces of silver.

Li was wealthy but he went away without giving him any, the priest, too, rising up in a rage and shouting after him, "I hope you won't repent."

Li went home, and found his son was already dead. He then pleaded the priest to help. In the evening, after dusk, Li was sitting alone with his wife, when suddenly a little boy was heard to say, "Dad! Why do you hurry on so fast? I couldn't catch you up."

Li was frightened, and ran away with his wife The boy calling after them, "Dad! Mom!"

Li asked the boy what he was up to, and the boy replied, "My name is Chan. I am six years of age and was left an orphan. My brother and my sister-in-law sent me to live at my maternal grandfather's. One day, when playing outside, a wicked priest killed me and turned me into an evil spirit. I would now remain with you as your son."

Li said, "We are human beings and you are a devil. How can we remain together?"

"Arrange me to stay in a tiny room," cried the boy, "a bed, and a cup of cold gruel every day. I ask for nothing more."

One day, Li he took Young Zhu's body home, and had hardly laid it on the bed when he noticed the boy's eyes move. Young Zhu then called for some broth, which put him into a perspiration, and then he got up.

Li and his wife were all overjoyed to see their son come to life again. To their surprise, the boy lay perfectly stiff and rigid, without showing any signs of life.

One day, Li's wife asked Young Zhu whether he had seen his sister, Xiaohui; and he said he had not, promising to go again and inquire about her. A few days later, he told his mother that Xiaohui was very happy in Purgatory, being married to a son of one of the Judge.

One day the boy ran in and cried out, "Mom, Xiaohui has come. We had better get plenty of wine ready." When the girl came, neither Li nor his wife saw their daughter.

Shortly after these events Li became dangerously ill, and no medicines were of any avail.

TALE 40
Silly Sun

Sun Zuchu in Guangxi was a scholar born with six fingers. Unlike many who hunted women in the street, he was a man who had a strange feeling about fair sex, and the sight of a woman was enough to send him flying in the opposite direction. His friends laughed heartily at his strange behavior. So he got the nickname of Silly Sun.

In the town where Sun resided, there was a rich trader whose connections were all highly aristocratic. He was not only wealthy but also had a daughter named A Pao. She was of great beauty, and the father was looking for husband for her.

Some of Silly Sun's friends joked Sun should try his luck. Sun had no idea of his own shortcomings, and proceeded at once to follow this advice. A Pao's father knew him to be an accomplished scholar, but rejected him on the ground of poverty.

When Silly Sun's go-between was leaving, he chanced to meet A Pao, and related to her the object of her visit.

A Pao laughed and said to the go-between, "I was told he has six fingers. If he'll cut off his extra finger, I'll marry him."

When Silly Sun was told of this, he seized a chopper, and cut one of his fingers clean off. He then asked the go-between to go and tell A Pao. Then the girl told the go-between to tell Silly Sun to try to cut off the "silly" from his reputation.

Sun ceased to trouble himself about her. During the Lunar New Year, Silly Sun's friends urged him to join them in their expedition, and one of them asked him with a smile if he wished to A Pao himself.

When A Pao came, the excitement among the young men was intense; and Silly Sun was the only to remain silent.

One day A Pao went to worship at the Shuiyue Temple, Silly Sun followed her in a great state of excitement. A Pao asked one of her maids to ask his name, and Silly Sun told her who he was. Strange enough, however, Silly Sun became very ill, and had to lie on his bed unconscious, without taking any food, occasionally calling on A Pao by name.

A Pao was greatly astonished at this. She and her mother found out that Silly Sun was actually well known as a clever fellow, but was desperately poor. Ultimately, her father and mother gave their consent.

When Sun was told the news, his illness rapidly disappeared. A Pao's father invited Sun to come and live with them after the marriage.

The marriage was then celebrated, and bride and bridegroom met as if for the first time in their lives. Unfortunately, Sun suddenly fell ill and died. Mrs. Sun was inconsolable, and refused either to sleep or take nourishment. One night, she hanged herself. Her maid, hearing a noise, ran in and cut her down just in time but she still steadily refused all food.

The friends and relatives of Sun came to attend his funeral for three days, when suddenly they heard a sigh proceeding forth from the coffin. The coffin was then opened and Sun had come to life again.

TALE 41

Zhen Xiu

One day, a man named Zhen Chinqi from Yutai met a man who told him his name was Shen Zhuting and a native of Shuchen. They soon became good friends and decided to travel together.

One day, Zhen fell sick and in ten days he gradually got worse. Finally, he had to say to Shen, "I am about to die. Now in my purse you will find two hundred ounces of silver. Take half, and when you have defrayed my funeral expenses, use the balance for your return journey, and give the other half to my family, that they may be able to send for my coffin."

He then, with the aid of a pillow, wrote a letter, and that evening he died.

It was more than a year before Zhen's family knew what had taken place. Zhen's son young Xiu was just about seventeen years of age, and had recently successfully passed the regional imperial examination. But he was a boy who loved gambling.

Finally, young Xiu went together with his uncle named Chang, who was going to the capital for business purpose.

When they reached Linqing, where the clear rattle of dice from a neighboring boat fell upon Xiu's ear, and before long he was itching to be back again at his old games.

While his uncle was fast asleep, he got up quietly with his money. Crossing over into the boat whence the sounds proceeded, he beheld two persons engaged in gambling for high stakes. As the play was in full swing another man walked in, and also asked to be allowed to join.

Now Xiu's uncle, waking up in the middle of the night, and knew at once where he was. He immediately followed him to the boat with a view of bringing him back. Finding that Xiu was a heavy winner, he said nothing to him, only carrying off a portion of his winnings to their own boat and making the others of his party get up and help him to fetch the rest, even then leaving behind a large sum for Xiu to go on with.

The proprietor of the gambling boat now found that the lumps of silver which he had changed for his customers were nothing more than so much tinsel, and rushing off in a great state of alarm to Xiu's boat, told him what had happened and asked him to make it good; but when he discovered he was speaking to the son of his former travelling companion, Zhen Chinqi, he hung his head and slunk away covered with shame.

So going into partnership with his uncle, they proceeded north together, and by the end of the year their capital had increased five-fold. Xiu became the richest man in that part of the country.

TALE 42

Two Brothers

A Chang from Shandong had a son named Na. When his wife was killed during a war, he married a Henan wife from the Niu family, who bore him a son named Cheng. Niu was a malicious woman who often beat young Na, and treated him like a house slave.

As Cheng grew up and began to understand the fraternal love, he hated to see what his mother did to his brother.

One day, when Na was asked to work in the mountain, a violent storm came on, and he took shelter under a cliff. It was getting dark and he began to feel very hungry. When he managed to reach home, his stepmother, displeased with the small quantity of wood he had brought, refused to give him anything to eat. When Cheng came back from school, and saw the state his brother Na was in, he offered some cakes to Na.

Cheng told Na, "I stole some flour and got a neighbor to make them for me. Eat away, and don't talk."

Na ate them up, but begged his brother not to do this again, as he might get himself into trouble.

Next day, after breakfast, Cheng went to the place where Na worked. He went there to help gather firewood. Na asked him to go back home but he refused.

One day, when Na and Cheng went with a number of others to cut wood, a tiger rushed down from the hills upon them. The tiger, seizing Cheng, ran off with him in his mouth.

Na, rushing after them, hacked away at the tiger's flanks with his axe. The Bain only made the tiger hurry off, and in a few minutes they were out of sight.

Na made a great chop at his own neck. The wound was over an inch deep, and blood was flowing so copiously that Na became faint, and seemed at the point of death.

His stepmother cursed him, "You have killed my son!"

In the village where these events took place there was a sorcerer employed in certain devil-work among mortals.

Na had been in a trance for two days, and when he recovered he was told Cheng was not dead. His mother, however, looked upon the story as a make-up, and never ceased reviling him. As he had no means of proving his innocence, and his neck was now quite healed, he got up from the bed and said to his father he was going away to seek for his brother.

A year had passed away before he reached Nanjing. He came across a gentleman of about forty, who appeared to be a mandarin, with numerous lusty attendants and fiery steeds accompanying him. One young man on a small palfrey, whom Na took to be the mandarin's son. The young man jump cried out, "Are you not my brother?"

Na raised his head, and found that Cheng stood before him. Grasping each other's hands, the brothers burst into tears. Na told him the whole story.

Wine and food were placed on the table; and while they

were chatting together the mandarin asked Na about the number of their family in Henan.

"There is only my father," replied Na, "and he is a Shandong man who came to live in Henan."

The mandarin happened to be a Shandong man too. Na told his mother was carried away by soldiers in Shandong. The mandarin went into the house.

In a few moments out came an old lady, who explained to Na and Cheng, "Three years after my marriage with your father, I was carried off to the north and made a slave in a mandarin's family. Six months afterwards your elder brother here was born, and in another six months the mandarin died. I have often thought of my native place. How should I know that he had gone to Henan?"

They then sold their house and packed up, and were soon on the way to Henan. When they arrived, Cheng went in first to tell his father, whose third wife had died since Na left. He was overjoyed to see Cheng again, and, looking fondly at his son, burst into tears.

Cheng told him his mother and brothers were outside.

TALE 43
Performing Mice

Aman from Chang'an lived by exhibiting performing mice. Whenever a performance was given, he let out some ten mice and he himself beat a drum while singing old theatrical melody. The mice would then dance.

The mice were smart enough to give a performance portraying the various emotions of joy and anger, exactly like human actors of either sex.

TALE 44

Xiangju's Misfortunes

An old man named Feng had an only son called Xiangju. The family had long been poor.

One night Xiangju was sitting out in the moonlight, when suddenly a young lady from next door got on the wall to have a look at him. As he approached her she began to laugh. The young lady said her name was Miss Hong Yu, and lived next door. Xiangju was much taken with her beauty and begged her to come over frequently and have a chat.

The girl agreed, and did so for several months, until one evening Feng discovered the meeting. He was angry, and shouted at his son, "We are very poor. Why aren't you at your books?"

With tears in eyes, Xiangju implored forgiveness. His father turned to Miss Hong Yu, and said, "If people find this out, we shall not be the only ones to suffer."

Hong Yu, weeping bitterly, said to Xiangju their friendship was at an end, but she told him to meet her again the following evening.

At the appointed time she arrived, and produced forty ounces of silver to Xiangju, telling him that to go and find a girl named Wei, eighteen years of age, who was not yet married and Xiangju should go and try his luck.

Xiangju's father had doubts because they were not sufficiently well off and urged him not to go. However, Xiangju finally persuaded his father and went.

When the father of Wei met Xiangju, he found Xiangju belonged to a very good family and when he saw all the retinue Xiangju had brought with him, he consented in mind to the match.

Xiangju emptied his purse on the table, and Mr. Wei was delighted. Xiangju then went in to pay his respects to Mrs. Wei, whom he found in a small, miserable room, with Miss Wei hiding behind her. Xiangju found the young lady herself was very nice-looking.

Xiangju and his wife Wei got alone very well. In two years she had a son called Fu Er. And once, on the occasion of the great spring festival, she chanced to meet a man named Sung, who was one of the gentry of the neighborhood.

When Mr. Sung saw Xiangju's wife, he was attracted by her beauty. He told Xiangju he would use land as compensation so as to have his wife. When Xiangju heard what was wanted, he was very angry.

His father got into a violent rage, but old Feng and his son were given a most tremendous beating. Xiangju's wife ran in, and, throwing her child down on the bed, tore her hair and shrieked for help. Sung's attendants carried her off, while there lay her husband and his father, wounded on the ground, and the baby squalling on the bed.

The neighbors came to their rescue. The father died and Xiangju was lived in tears.

One day a personage of striking appearance came to condole with him on his losses. The stranger said to Xiangju, "Have you forgotten your father's death, your wife's disgrace?"

Xiangju, suspecting him to be a spy from the Sung family, made some evasive reply, which so irritated the stranger that he roared out, "Be a man!"

Xiangju fell on his knees and implored the stranger to forgive him.

When night came, and the members of the Sung family were wrapped in sleep, someone found his way into their house and slew Sung and his two sons, besides a maid-servant and one of the ladies. The Sung family had no doubt that the murderer was Xiangju, and the magistrate sent out people to arrest him.

Xiangju, however, was nowhere to be found, a fact which tended to confirm the suspicions of the Sung family. Finally, Xiangju was found and taken to the court.

Xiangju was then stripped of his official degrees and subjected to all kinds of indignities, but they were unable to wring a confession from his lips.

That very night, as the magistrate lay down, he found a keen blade sticking in the wood at the head of his couch so tightly that it could not be drawn out. Terribly alarmed at this, the magistrate walked round the room with a spear over his shoulder, but without finding anything. He quickly ordered to have Xiangju released from the jail.

TALE 45
Life-and-Death Marriage

Magistrate Zheng of Sanhan County had a daughter who was very fond of hunting. One day when she went hunting, she came across a young man named Chang, who pursued his studies at the Xiao Temple. She was dressed in an embroidered sable jacket, and rode about on a small palfrey. Chang instantly fell in love with her.

Chang had the young lady in his mind but he was later told girl Zheng had died suddenly, and her father deposited the coffin in a temple where Chang was residing.

From then on, Chang often went to pay respects to her remains. When some six months later, one night the young man saw a young lady standing, all smiles, before him.

"Thank you very much for your love of me, I was unable to resist the temptation of coming to thank you myself," said girl Zheng.

From then on, the young lady came every evening. One night, she aid to Chang, "I used to be very fond of riding and archery, shooting the games. My crime is so great that I can find no repose in death. I pray you recite for me the Diamond Sutra five thousand and forty-eight times so as to help redeem my sin." Chang did as he was asked from then on.

One night, he told girl Zheng he wished to visit his parents and hoped to take her with him.

Five years later, Miss Zheng's father lost her job and was so poor that he could not afford to pay for the removal of his daughter's coffin and wanted to bury it economically where it was. Chang said that a friend of his had a piece of waste land near the temple, and that he might bury it there. Chang assisted him with the funeral.

One night after this, as Miss Zheng came for a visit and she burst into a flood of tears, saying, "The sum of my Sutras is complete, and today I am to be born again in the family of a high-ranking official named Lu Hepei. Meet me there in fifteen years from now, on the 16th of the 8th moon."

Chang promised he would remember it.

That official Lu Hepei had a daughter. When she was born, she could talk. Very clever and beautiful as she grew up, she was the idol of her parents, and had been asked in marriage by many suitors, but would not accept any of them. When asked why, she told them the story of her engagement in her former life.

One day, Chang arrived for a visit, but the doorkeeper would not let him in. Meanwhile girl Zheng thought that he had broken his engagement, and refused all food.

When Mr. Lu went out to meet Chang in the fields, the old man found quite a young man. Mr. Lu was so charmed with his young friend's bearing that he invited him to his house. However, the girl had died a sudden death.

That night, Chang dreamed that she appeared to him, and said, "I have already died from grief; but if you make haste to the little street shrine and summon my spirit back, I may still recover. Be not late!"

Chang found that the young lady had been dead two days. Telling her father his dream, they went forth to summon the spirit back. On opening the shroud, a noise was heard in the young lady's throat, and her lips parted. They moved her onto a bed, and soon she began to moan, to the great joy of Mr. Lu, who took Chang out of the room and they had a good chat. The old man was glad to find that Chang was a suitable match for his daughter, and an auspicious day was fixed for the wedding.

TALE 46

The Fox Spirit

Wang Muzhen was from a rich family in Mengyin County, Shandong. When he was visiting Zhejiang one day, he found an old lady crying by the roadside and went up to find out why. She said, "Before my husband's death we had a son who is now imprisoned for committing a crime. Who can help him?" Wang Muzhen had always wanted to help people so he memorized the name of her son. He used his money to facilitate things and her son was acquitted and released. When the man came out of prison and learned how Wang Muzhen had saved his life, he could not understand why Wang had done so. He went to visit Wang at his hotel, thanked him and asked why. Wang Muzhen said, "I helped you because I pitied your mother." The man was surprised, saying, "My mother died years ago." Now it was Wang Muzhen who was surprised. In the evening, the old lady came and Wang Muzhen asked her why she had told a lie. She said, "To be honest, I am a fox from the East Mountain and had a one-night affair with the man's father twenty years ago. I did not want to see my one-night husband's son die." Wang was impressed by her loyalty and before he could ask any more questions, she had disappeared.

Wang Muzhen's wife was a kind-hearted woman and a Buddhist disciple. She was so pious that she did not drink nor had meat. She put aside a room, kept it clean and had a portrait of the Goddess of Mercy hung on the wall. Since she had given birth to no son, she prayed in the room all day long. The goddess often helped people, instructing Wang's wife to avoid disasters and so the family lived in harmony and peace. In fact, whatever the wife did, she did according to the will of the goddess. Later the woman had fallen ill seriously. She had a bed moved into the prayer room, put aside another set of bedding in the same room and had the door locked, as if she was waiting to share the room with somebody else. Wang could not understand what was going on, but since his wife was very ill, he did not want to press her for an answer. His wife lay in bed for two years. Afraid of any sound, she insisted that she would sleep all by herself. She was, however, often heard talking with somebody inside the prayer room. When her room was opened, Wang found no one except his wife. Wang's wife had a daughter fourteen yams old, and in her sick bed, she urged her husband to marry their daughter off. When she was married, Wang's wife held his hand and said, "I'm going to die now. When I first got sick, the Goddess of Mercy told me that I wouldn't have much time. At the time, I was worried about our daughter's marriage, so the goddess gave me some medicine to prolong my life. Last year, before the goddess left for the South Sea, she left her maid Xiaomei to look after me. I'm an unfortunate person and will die soon, without giving birth to a son for you. But I love Baor. I am afraid after my death, you will marry again and your wife may not be kind enough to Baor and his mother. Since Xiaomei is beautiful and kind, please take her as your step-wife." Wang Muzhen had a concubine who had given birth to a boy named Baor. Wang Muzhen found his wife's words very strange, so he said, "You've been very devoted to the Goddess of Mercy and is what you've said just now a disrespect?" His wife said, "Xiaomei has been with me for more than a year, and we are close and know each other extremely well. I've asked her to marry you." Wang Muzhen asked, "Where is Xiaomei then?" His wife said, "Don't you see she is right in this room?" Before he could ask again, his wife was already dead.

That night, Wang kept vigil for his wife and suddenly heard somebody sobbing, which greatly alarmed him as he thought there must be a ghost. He had his wife's room unlocked and saw a beautiful girl about fifteen or sixteen years old wearing a mourning dress. People thought they were seeing a spirit and knelt down, bowing. The young woman forced back her tears and helped them up. Wang Muzhen watched on the side and found the woman not saying anything. So he said, "If what my wife told me before her death is right, please come into the main room and accept the show of respect of the children. If you don't agree, then I won't cherish any wishful thinking." Now blushed, the young woman came out and walked into the main hall. Wang had a maid place a chair for her and he was the first to bow to her. She returned his bow out of respect. Then, the entire household knelt down and kowtowed to her according to seniority. The young woman sat there solemnly accepting the show of respect. When Wang Muzhen's concubine came to kneel down, the young woman immediately help her up.

Ever since Wang's ex-wife fell ill, the servants in the house had become sloppy and the household had gone downhill. Now the servants bowed and stood on both sides. Xiaomei, the young woman, began to speak, "I was grateful for Mrs. Wang's kindness, so I decided to stay. Now she has entrusted the whole family to me. From today on all of you should bid goodbye to your past behavior and serve the master whole-heartedly. This way I will not punish you for what you have done in the past. Don't think there is no housewife under this roof." They all looked at her and found her sitting there just like the goddess in the portrait. Holding her in awe, they promised to do as she had said. So Xiaomei made the funeral arrangements, assigning them to different jobs and none were lax in their duties.

Xiaomei ran the house well, and whatever Wang Muzhen did, he had to consult her first. Though they saw each other every night, there was no talk of an intimate relationship. After Wang's wife was properly buried, he wanted to fulfill what had been promised between him and Xiaomei, but did not want to say it directly to her himself. So he sent his concubine to suggest it to Xiaomei, who said, "Since I have accepted Mrs. Wang's arrangement, I have the obligation to carry it out. But marriage is a solemn thing and has to be done properly. Your uncle Mr. Wang is a highly respected man. Ask him to preside over our wedding and I will do what I have promised." Mr. Huang from Xinshui County had been a high-ranking official, but now lived in retirement. He had been a close friend of Wang Muzhen's father. Wang therefore personally went to see Mr. Huang and told him everything. Surprised by what he heard, Mr. Huang came with Wang to his house. Xiaomei hurriedly ran out to kneel in front of Mr. Huang by way of welcome. Huang thought he had seen an angel and did not dare to accept her bow. We decided to pay expensive dowries for her and did not go back home until he had performed his duty at the wedding. Xiaomei gave Mr. Huang pillows and shoes that she had made by herself and treated Mr. Huang as if he were her father-in-law. So this way the two families became very close.

When they married, Wang Muzhen always regarded Xiao-mei, his new wife, as a spirit and was rather reserved when they were most intimate together. He often asked her about the details of the life of the Goddess of Mercy. Xiaomei smiled, saying, "Don't be silly. When did you ever hear of a goddess marrying a secular man?" Wang Muzhen kept asking her about her history. She told him, "Don't try to press me. Since you treat me like I am a god, do so day and night and you'll be free of disasters." Towards the servants, Xiaomei was very kind, smiling all the time, but when they saw her at a distance, they grew quiet. Xiaomei tried to persuade them, "Do you think I'm a spirit? Of course, I'm not. Actually I am a cousin of Mrs. Wang. When she was sick, she sent for me. Since it was not appropriate for me to mix around with my brother-in-law, I pretended to be a spirit and stayed inside my sister's room all the time. I am no spirit!" Nobody believed her. As they found her behavior just like an ordinary lady, gradually the talk about her being a spirit died down. The most difficult servants whom Wang Muzhen could not keep under control either by swearing or beating all followed what Xiaomei said. They said, "We don't know how to explain it. It is not fear of the mistress, but we become soft as soon as we see her face. So we don't think it is right to do things against her will." Things were back on track at Mr. Wang's house and in several years' time, the Wangs had their land expanded and granaries filled with grain.

Several years later, Xiaomei gave birth to a son who had a red mole on his left arm, winning him the nickname Red Mole. When he was a month old, Xiaomei had Wang Muzhen prepare a feast to entertain Mr. Huang. The old man sent expensive gifts but declined to come, reasoning he was too old to travel far. Xiaomei sent two maids to invite Mr. Huang again, who eventually had to come. Xiaomei showed him her son, asking him to explain what the red mole meant. Mr. Huang smiled, saying, "This is a lucky red mole and I think we should call him Lucky Red Mole." Xiaomei was delighted and kowtowed to Mr. Huang. That day, the whole house was filled with music and guests. Mr. Huang stayed for three days before he left for home.

One day, a horse-drawn cart suddenly arrived outside the house to pick up Xiaomei for a visit home. For more than ten years, no relatives of Xiaomei had ever come to visit her and the sudden arrival of the cart had everybody talking. Xiaomei, however, offered no explanation. She carefully did her make-up, got dressed and took her son in her arms. She asked Wang Muzhen to see them off. After they were about fifteen kilometers away from home and when there was not a single person in sight, Xiaomei stopped the cart and asked Wang Muzhen to get off. She told the servants to stand away and whispered to Wang, "My husband! Our life together is short and our separation is long. Isn't this a tragedy?" Wang was taken aback and asked her what she really meant. Xiaomei said, "Can you tell me who you think I really am?" Wang said he could not answer that. Xiaomei told him, "Once you saved a man from being sentenced to death in the south. Is that true?" Wang said "yes." Xiaomei went on, "The old lady who cried by the roadside was my mother. She was deeply moved by your benevolence and wanted to pay you back. So she made use of your wife's devotion to the Goddess of Mercy and took the opportunity to send me over to thank you. Now that we have a baby son, I have done what mother wanted me to do. I realize your good days arc running out and it will be hard for the boy to continue to live here. So I am taking him away from trouble. Please remember if somebody dies in the family, go to the Willow Dike on the West River when the rooster crows. If you see somebody holding a sunflower lamp, stop him and beg him for help. That way you will be free from disasters." Wang Muzhen nodded and asked Xiaomei when she would be back. Xiaomei said, "This is hard to predict. Please remember what I've said and it won't be too long before we meet again." They held each other's hands and bid goodbye with tears in their eyes. She jumped onto the cart and drove off. Wang Muzhen watched until the cart had totally disappeared before he turned homeward.

Six to seven years had passed without any news from Xiaomei. Suddenly a strange disease broke out in the village and many people died. A maid in Mr. Wang's house was caught by the illness and died three days later. Wang, remembering Xiaomei's instruction, grew concerned. One day, after he became very drunk while drinking with some guests, he dozed off soundly. When he woke up, he heard a rooster crowing. He got up and ran toward the Willow Dike, where he found a lantern being taken away. It was about one hundred steps away, so he ran after it. The more he ran, the further away the lantern became and later it simply was out of sight. He had to go back home with regret. Several days later, he became ill and died. Most of the members of the Wang clan were shameless rascals who began to bully Wang's concubine and her children, openly harvesting her crops and felling her trees. Wang Muzhen's family began to grow poor. A year later, Baor, her first child with Wang Muzhen, died. With the boy dead, the clan members became more aggressive, dividing the land and taking away the domestic animals. They even planned to divide up the houses. One day they came with a group of people who tried to take the concubine out of the house to sell her. She clutched to her daughter, crying in despair. Her neighbors were saddened by what they saw.

Just then a sedan chair arrived outside the house and out from it came Xiaomei and her son. She looked around at the crowd and asked, "Who are these people?" The concubine told her what had happened while still crying. Xiaomei's face became grim and she told the servant to lock the door with a huge lock. The clan members wanted to protest but found themselves unable to make a move. Xiaomei had each one tied to a pillar of the corridor, feeding them with three bowls of thin porridge a day. Immediately she sent for Mr. Huang. Once inside the house, she cried. Then she said to the concubine, "This is purely fate. I planned to be back a month ago but my mother was suddenly sick. Little did I expect to see that our family had fallen to what it is today!" She asked about the maids and learned that they had been forcibly taken away by clan members. The next day, they came back, having learned that the hostess had returned. They cried violently when they met.

The shameless rascals tied to the corridor pillars insisted that the boy Xiaomei brought back was not Wang Muzhen's son. Xiaomei did not argue with them. When Mr. Huang came, she took Lucky Red Mole to greet him. Mr. Huang held the boy's left arm, rolled up the sleeve and pointed out the red mole to people around, verifying that he was indeed Wang Muzhen's son. Then he checked what property was missing, put them down on a list and went to visit the county magistrate who next had the rascals arrested and lashed forty times, telling them to pay back what they had taken away. Several days later, all the animals and land were returned to the former openers.

Mr. Huang was about to leave, Xiaomei thanked him. Crying, she said, "I'm not a human being of this world and Uncle Huang of course knew this all along. Now please take the boy with you." Mr. Huang promised, "As long as I live, I will do everything for the boy." After he was gone, Xiaomei entrusted Lucky Red Mole to the concubine and she went to her husband's tomb to pay her respects, taking along food and wine as sacrifices. A long time passed and she did not return home. People were sent out to look for her and they bound the sacrificial items right there in front of the tomb, but she was nowhere to be seen.

TALE 47

Fighting the Fox Spirits

One day, a scholar named Hu went to a wealthy family in Chili, which was to employ a tutor. Both parties were satisfied with each other.

Tutor Hu was very fond of roaming around in the wild, and generally came back in the middle of the night. As he entered the house without having to knock if the door was locked, it was therefore suspected that he was a fox spirit.

Tutor Hu found his master had a daughter. One day he went off for a holiday, and on the next day a stranger called; who, tying a black mule at the door, accepted the invitation of the master to take a seat within.

When the stranger was told about the conditions for the match, he got very angry, and his host also lost his temper. They came to high words, and were already on the way to blows, when the latter ordered his servants to give the stranger a beating and turn him out.

The stranger retired, leaving his mule behind him. They tried to lead it away, but it would not move; and on giving it a shove with the hand from behind, it toppled over and was discovered to be only of straw.

Sure enough the next day a whole host of fox soldiers arrived. The foxes shouted out and set the place on fire. Just then one of the servants rushed forward to engage the foxes. Stones and arrows flew about in all directions, and many on both sides were wounded. The foxes drew off, leaving their swords on the field. These glittered like frost or snow, but when picked up turned out to be only millet stalks.

Next day, they were deliberating together, when suddenly a giant descended upon them from the sky. More than ten feet high, he brandished a sword as broad as half a door. He was soon be killed, and found that he was made of grass.

The attackers began to make light of the fox attackers. The fox fighters soon reappeared. Armed with bows and arrows, they succeeded in shooting the master of the house in the back.

When the arrow was pulled out from the back of the house master, it was found to be nothing but a long thorn. This annoyed the master of the family very much.

One day, Tutor Hu appeared at the head of a troop of fox soldiers. The fox soldiers were ready to discharge their arrows when Hu stopped them.

The master invited Hu into the house and treated him with good wine.

"Mr. Hu, I trust you, but my daughter is still a great deal too young. There is my son whom you have taught. He is fifteen years old, and I should be proud to see him connected with you."

Hu was delighted, and said, "I have a daughter one year younger than your son; she is neither ugly nor stupid."

They then became the best of friends, forgetting all about what had happened.

From then on, there was no more trouble and a year passed without any news of Hu, so that it seemed as if he wished to get out of the business.

However, a few more months later, Hu reappeared and requested that an auspicious day might be fixed for his daughter to be married to his son.

This being arranged, the young lady arrived with a retinue of sedan chairs, and horses, and a beautiful trousseau that nearly filled a room. She was unusually respectful to her parents-in-law. Her father, Hu or the tutor, often came to visit her in her new home.

TALE 48
Fox Thief

A family in Nanyang, Henan, with the surname E, knew there was a fox spirit in their home as the family's jewelry and other objects were often stolen. If the family did not allow it to do what it liked, it would simply make more trouble.

Mr. E had a grandson named Ji who burned incense to pray to the fox spirit not to make trouble, but his efforts were in vain. He also begged the fox spirit not to stay at his grandfather's home and invited it to his home, still the fox spirit refused him. People laughed at him but Ji reasoned, "Foxes are very fickle, so they must have some human nature. I would like to guide them and make them behave better." Every few days, he would pray in E's house. Though there were no visible results, the fox spirit did stop making trouble whenever Ji came. So Mr. E often asked Ji to stay for the night. At night, Ji looked at the sky and more sincerely invited the fox spirit to come and meet him.

One day Ji sat alone in his study. Suddenly the door opened on its own. Ji stood up in the proper way of greeting a visitor and said, "Is that you, Brother Fox?" His question was met by silence.

Another night, the door opened again. Ji said, "If you are here, Brother Fox, why don't you come out since I have invited you so many times?" Again there was only silence, but the money Ji had put on the desk was no longer there in the morning. In the evening, Ji put out more money on the desk. At midnight, there was a sound from the bed net. Ji asked, "Are you here now? I have prepared some money for you. I am not rich but not tight-fisted either. If you need money, please tell me straight forward. Why do you have to steal it?" Still some of the money disappeared. Ji left the remaining money in the same place, but for several days, it stayed where it was. Ji had cooked a chicken to be used to entertain some guests and it disappeared. In the evening, Ji put out some wine, but the fox spirit did not show up and take it. The E house was still troubled by the thefts. Ji went there to pray again, saying, "I have prepared some money for you, but you did not take it. I have prepared some wine for you and you didn't drink it. My grandfather is old and weak. Please do not come to his place to make any more trouble. I shall prepare some small gifts and please help yourself to them tonight." Then he put some money, wine and some chicken on the desk. Ji slept next to the gifts. For the whole night, there was not a single sound, and the money and food were untouched. The fox spirit did not make any trouble after that.

One evening when Ji reached home, he found a pot of wine on the desk in his study, a plate of chicken and some money tied with a red string. He knew these were from the fox spirit. The wine smelled good, but it was green. Ji was half drunk after he finished the pot of wine. Then he was struck by a greedy idea and felt compelled to steal something. He went outside and decided to go to the home of a rich family in the village. He climbed over the wall into the courtyard. Though the wall was tall, Ji jumped over it easily, as if he had a pair of wings. In the house, he took fur coats and gold objects, which he left at his bedside in his study when he went to sleep. During the day, he took the stolen objects into his bedroom. His wife was surprised to see them and asked him where he had got them. He told her the exciting story, but his wife was frightened, saying, "You've always been honest and straightforward, how come you have become a thief?" Ji was at ease and did not find his behavior strange. He told her about his good relationship with the fox spirit. It then dawned on his wife who said, "The wine you drank must have poisons from the fox spirit!" She remembered that cinnabar could help rid a person of such poisons. She crushed some and put it in wine for Ji to drink. A little while later, Ji shouted suddenly, "How could I have stolen these things?" His wife explained what had happened to him patiently and Ji seemed at a loss as what to do. He heard the news about the rich man being robbed. Everyone in the village knew the story. Ji had no appetite for food or drink. His wife worked out a plan and told him to throw the stolen objects into the rich family's courtyard at night. Ji did according to his wife's suggestion and the situation calmed down after the rich family found their stolen objects had been returned.

That year saw Ji finishing first in the imperial exams and winning a special reward for his good behavior and morality. On the day the award was granted, a poster appeared on a high beam of a building in the government office announcing, "Mr. Ji was a thief. He stole a fur coat and golden objects from a rich family. How can he be regarded as a well-behaved person?" The beam was very tall and the poster could not have been put up by a man, even standing on his toes. This poster was taken down and shown to Ji, who was surprised. He thought that apart from his wife nobody knew about this. Besides, no human beings could enter the heavily guarded government office and put up the poster. He realized it must be the doing of the fox spirit. He told the entire story. The government encouraged him again by granting him another award for his honesty.

Ji thought he had never harmed the fox spirit, but the fox spirit often made trouble for him. It must be the case in which a lowly person intending to harm Ji was too ashamed to do it himself and so he had the fox spirit do it for him.

TALE 49

Life and Death in Thunder-storms

Yu Xiaosi, a native of Dongchang County, Shandong, was involved in the warehousing business. Xiashi, his wife, one day came back from her mother's home and saw an old lady with a young girl weeping sadly outside her house. Xiashi found that the woman's husband was Wang Xinzhai, an offspring of a rich official. The family went broke and had no food and clothes. They asked someone to be their guarantor to borrow some money from a rich family by the name of Huang, but they were robbed of the borrowed money. It was fortunate that the robbers had not taken their lives. Soon after they returned home, Huang came to ask them to pay back the debts. By then they had nothing left to either pay back the debt or to offer as a guarantee. Mr. Huang found Renzhen, Wang's daughter, a young and beautiful girl, so he wanted to take her as his concubine. He sent a message to the family saying he would forgive the debt if they agreed to send him their daughter. In addition, Huang agreed to pay them twenty taels of silver as a deposit for Renzhen. When Wang Xinzhai discussed this with his wife, she wept, "We are poor but we are the offspring of a rich official. Mr. Huang became rich by driving a cart. How dare he buy my daughter as his concubine! And furthermore, we have already agreed to marry Renzhen to someone else."

Scholar Fu's son was a good friend of Wang Xinzhai. When his wife gave birth to a baby boy named A'mao, the parents arranged the marriage of A'mao and Renzhen. Fu was later appointed an official in Fujian and died a year after he took the post. His wife and children, including Renzhen's future husband, were unable to come back to their hometown and there was no news about them. In fact because of this early marriage pledge, Renzhen was still not married at the age of fifteen.

Wang Xinzhai racked his brains to come up with an idea. His wife said, "If there is no other way, I shall go and discuss this with my two brothers." The wife's maiden name was Fan. Her grandfather was once an official in the capital and had left a great deal of land to his sons and grandsons. The next day, Wang's wife met with her two younger brothers at her mother's home. The two brothers listened, but did not offer any help. Fanshi had to go back home, empty handed. She could not control her tears as she went home. That was when she met Xiashi near Xiashi's house. So still sobbing, she again told the story. Xiashi took pity on her. When she saw how beautiful the woman's daughter was, she took even greater pity on them and asked them to come to her home. Xiashi comforted them, saying, "Don't be sad. I shall try my best to help." Renzhen cried and knelt on the ground to thank her. Xiashi told them, "I have some savings, but thirty taels of silver is still not enough. I shall sell some belongings to give you more money." The mother and daughter left, comforted and very grateful. Xiashi told them to come to her home and pick up the money in three days. After they left, Xiashi thought hard to find ways to come up with the money, but she dared not tell her husband. On the third day, she still did not have enough money and so she sent a servant to borrow the money from her mother. When Fanshi and her daughter arrived, Xiashi told them the situation and asked them to return the following day. Later that afternoon, Xiashi wrapped up her own money and the borrowed money in a package and left it at her bedside. At night, a burglar sneaked into her home. Xiashi was terrified by the very fierce-looking man with a knife. She did not utter a word and pretended to sleep. The thief walked to a chest and tried to unlock it, but when he saw the package at Xiashi's bedside, he took it. He opened the package, put the money into his pocket and left without bothering to unlock the chest. Xiashi then shouted for help but there was only one maid at home. By the time their neighbors heard the commotion and arrived to help, the thief had got clean away.

Xiashi cried under the lamp. When she found the maid in deep sleep, she found a piece of rope and committed suicide by hanging herself on the window frame. The maid found her at daybreak and shouted for help, but Xiashi's body was already cold. Her husband, Yu Xiaosi, immediately came back and cried in deep grief. It was summer, but Xiashi's body did not rot, although it was not buried until seven days after her death.

After Xiashi was buried, Renzhen came to her tomb and cried. Suddenly there was a thunderstorm. In the flash of lightning, the wall of the tomb cracked. Renzhen died on the spot. After Yu Xiaosi learned of this, he went to the tomb and found the coffin open and his wife groaning inside. Yu Xiaosi carried her out, but did not recognize the woman lying beside his wife's coffin. Xiashi looked down and recognized Renzhen. At a loss to explain what had happened, they stood by the grave until Fanshi, the girl's mother, arrived and found her daughter. She said, "I guessed she was here. When she heard that Xiashi had committed suicide, she cried for an entire night. Tonight she told me that she would cry for Xiashi at her tomb. I did not agree, but she still came." Xiashi was moved by Renzhen and told her husband to bury Renzhen in her coffin. After the burial, Fanshi left and Yu Xiaosi carried his wife home. Fanshi told the story to her husband when she arrived at home.

Later, Fanshi heard that someone was struck dead by a bolt of lightning on the county road. On his body were written the words "The thief who stole Xiashi's money." She heard her neighbor crying and realized the dead man was her husband Ma Da. The villagers reported this to the court and they interrogated Ma Da's wife. What happened was that Fanshi was moved to tears when Xiashi promised to provide her and Renzhen with the money. This was overheard by Ma Da, a rascal and gambler, who decided to steal the money. The court investigators found twenty taels of silver at Ma Da's home and another four taels on Ma's body. The court decided to sell Ma Da's wife so that the thirty taels of silver could be paid back to Yu and Xiashi. Xiashi was glad and sent all the silver to Fanshi, asking her to pay back her creditor.

On the third day after Renzhen was buried, another strong thunderstorm opened the tomb and brought Renzhen back to life. She did not go to her own home, but went to knock at Xiashi's door. Xiashi, awakened, asked through the door who was knocking. Renzhen asked, "Are you alive? I'm Renzhen." Xiashi was afraid she was a spirit and asked her neighbor to check the door for her. They found it was Renzhen, who had come to life again, and Xiashi immediately let her into her house. Renzhen said, "I would like to work for you instead of going home." Xiashi told her, "Does it look as if I am buying a maid? After you were buried, your family's debts were paid off, so don't have any ideas like that." Renzhen was moved to tears and said she would like to treat Xiashi as her mother. Xiashi did not agree. Renzhen insisted, "I am able to work. I won't sit around and do nothing." Fanshi heard the news and came to see her daughter. She agreed to her daughter's idea of staying with Xiashi. After Fanshi left, Xiashi sent Renzhen to her own home. Renzhen missed Xiashi very much, so her father, Wang Xinzhai, took his daughter to the Yu house and left her with Xiashi. When Xiashi saw Renzhen and was told the reason, she decided to let her stay. Renzhen knelt down and bowed to Yu Xiaosi, calling him father. When Yu Xiaosi, who had no children, saw how lovely Renzhen was, he became very fond of her. Renzhen was diligent, sewing and weaving. When Xiashi fell seriously ill, Renzhen looked after her day and night. When Xiashi could not eat, she would not eat either. She often wept and said to others, "If my mother dies, I don't want to live either." When Xiashi took a turn for the better, Renzhen rejoiced. Xiashi was moved by this and said with tears, "I have no son though I'm already forty. If only I had a daughter like Renzhen, I would be very happy." Within a year, Xiashi gave birth to a baby boy. Everybody said that was a reward for her kindness.

Renzhen was now two years older. Yu Xiaosi and Wang Xinzhai discussed plans for her to marry. Wang Xinzhai said, "My daughter is at your home, so you should make the decisions for her." Renzhen was seventeen, beautiful and kindhearted. After the news about the intention of marrying her passed around, go-betweens lined up to visit the family. The couple had many choices. Mr. Huang, once the creditor, also sent over people to propose for his son. Yu Xiaosi resolutely rejected him as he thought that Huang was rich but unkind. Finally a man named Feng was chosen as Feng's father was a famous scholar and Feng was bright and good at writing compositions. Yu Xiaosi wanted to discuss this with Wang Xinzhai, but Wang was away on business. Yu made the decision by himself and agreed to the marriage. After Huang was refused by Yu, he went to Wang Xinzhai's home with the excuse of discussing business deals. He invited Wang to dine out and lent money to Wang to assist in his business. Huang told Wang Xinzhai how bright his son was and proposed to marry his son to Renzhen. Wang Xinzhai was grateful to him and admired Huang for his wealth, so he agreed to his daughter's marriage with Huang's son.

Wang Xinzhai went to Yu's house, but Yu Xiaosi had accepted Feng's proposal of marriage a day earlier. He was saddened after hearing what Wang Xinzhai had to say. He asked Renzhen to come out and told her the actual situation. Renzhen immediately became angry and said, "Huang was the creditor and is my enemy. If I am asked to look after my enemy, I would rather die." Wang Xinzhai realized that he had been wrong, so he asked a messenger to inform the Huangs that an agreement had already been reached with the Feng family. Huang said angrily, "The girl is named Wang, not Yu. I made the proposal before Feng. Why can't they keep their word?" He sued Wang in the county court. The court realized Huang had made the marriage proposal earlier, and so in this sense was entitled to the girl's hand. Feng argued, "Wang Xinzhai gave his daughter to the Yus and agreed not to interfere with his daughter's marriage. Furthermore, we have signed the intent of marriage. What do they have? Just an idea hatched in the bottom of a wine bottle." It was difficult for the court to make any decision and the court arranged to hear Renzhen's thoughts on the subject. Huang bribed the county officials and so the case dragged on for more than a month without a final decision.

One day a scholar was on his way to the north to take part in the imperial examinations when his cart passed by Dongchang County. He sent someone to look for Wang Xinzhai. It so happened that Yu was the man he met and asked about Wang Xinzhai. Yu Xiaosi found out from the person that the traveling scholar was named Fu. It was A'mao, who had come from Fujian on his way to the capital. As he had a marriage agreement with Renzhen dating to their childhood, he had remained single. His mother asked him to look for Wang Xinzhai and to see if his daughter had married. Yu Xiaosi was very happy to hear this and invited A'mao to his home, telling him Renzhen's story. Since this self-acclaimed son-in-law came from a thousand kilometers away, Yu wanted to see some proof of his identity. Fu A'mao opened a suitcase and showed him a written marriage agreement. Yu Xiaosi asked Wang Xinzhai to examine it and he found it to be authentic. Everybody was happy with this development. The court reexamined case. Fu A'mao visited the court officials and the case was easily settled. After the wedding date was selected, Fu A'mao left for the exams.

After the examinations, Fu A'mao bought some wedding gifts and stayed at his family's old house until the wedding ceremony. The good news that he had passed the imperial exams reached Fujian and then was passed on to Dongchang, where the wedding was to be held. Fu A'mao soon received an appointment in the ministry of rites. He went to the capital again and returned to Renzhen after finishing his work there. Renzhen did not want to go to Fujian and A'mao also thought that since Dongchang was where his ancestors were buried, he should make it his home. He went to Fujian alone to transfer his father's coffin and escort his mother back to his hometown in Dongchang, Shandong.

Yu Xiaosi died several years later, leaving a seven-year-old son. Renzhen treated him better than her own brother. She saw to it that he went to a proper school. The family became rich with Fu A'mao's help.

TALE 50
Sixteen Years on Fairy Island

Yang Yuedan, a scholar from Qiongzhou in Guangdong, traveled home by boat. On his way, he was caught in the middle of a storm. The boat was about to capsize when suddenly an empty boat appeared. He jumped onto the empty boat and saw the other boat capsize and the passengers drown. The wind continued to grow stronger and stronger. He had to close his eyes and let the wind blow him anywhere it wished.

In a short while, the sea calmed down. Yang Yuedan opened his eyes and found an island with many houses. He rowed the boat ashore and walked into the village. All was still. He heard no sounds of life, not even a chicken or dog. Then he saw a doorway lined with bamboos and pine trees on both sides. It was the beginning of winter, but a tree in the courtyard was blossoming. He was happy to see the beautiful flowers and hesitantly stepped closer. Suddenly he heard music coming from a distance. As he stood listening, a maid appeared. About fourteen years old, she was very beautiful. Then she saw Yang Yuedan, she turned away and quickly fled. The music stopped abruptly. A young man came out and asked where Yang Yuedan had come from. After Yang Yuedan answered, the young man asked about his hometown, family origins, and other personal items. Then the young man said happily, "Why, we are relatives!" He invited Yang to go inside an elegant house in the courtyard. At this moment, the music started again. A young girl of eighteen or nineteen years was adjusting her instrument. She looked extremely beautiful. When she saw Yang Yuedan, she immediately wanted to leave. The young man stopped her, saying, "Don't go away. He is a relative of your family." He told her about Yang Yuedan. The young lady said, "So, you are my nephew." She then asked, "Is grandma still healthy? How old are your parents?" Yang answered, "My parents are in their forties and in good health. Grandma is sixty years old and her health is not that good. She cannot walk by herself. Please tell me which aunt of mine you are so that I can tell my family members." The young lady said, "There has been no news as we are so far apart. Please tell your father that his tenth aunt is sending him her regards. He will know." Yang also asked the name of her husband. The young man answered for her as he said, "My name is Yan Haiyu. This place is called Fairy Island and is 1,500 kilometers from Qiongzhou. I haven't lived here for long." The girl, Shiniang, went inside asking her maids to prepare a meal to entertain the guest. The sea food and vegetables were delicious, but it was hard to tell the names of the different dishes.

After the meal, they walked about the island. Yang Yuedan saw peach and apricot trees laden with buds about to blossom and was surprised. Yan Haiyu explained to him, "It is neither hot in summer nor cold in winter here. The four seasons see flowers all the year around." Yang Yuedan admired, "This is indeed a fairy-land. When I go back home, I shall ask my parents to move here to be your neighbors." Yan Haiyu smiled. After they went back to the study, candles were lit and a musical instrument was placed on the desk. Yang Yuedan asked him to play a piece of music and Yan Haiyu adjusted the instrument and was about to start playing. Just at that moment, Shiniang came in. Yan Haiyu said, "Come along. Play for your nephew." Shiniang asked him, "What would you like to hear?" Yang Yuedan said, "I've never read the book Musical Practices and really don't know which pieces I would like." Shiniang said, "You can name any topic and I can play a piece fitting the topic." Yang Yuedan said with a smile. "The Sea Wind Guiding a Boat.' Can you play a piece fitting that title?" Shiniang assured him she could. She played improvisational notes, but the music was incredibly beautiful. It sounded like sea waves violently rocking a small boat. Yang Yuedan was surprised and asked, "Can I learn this?" Shiniang handed him the instrument and let him try. "I can teach you. What do you want to learn?" Yang Yuedan asked, "How long will it take to learn the music you played just now? Please write down the notes for me to remember." Shiniang answered, "There were no notes. I played according to my thoughts." She produced another musical instrument and asked him to imitate her. Yang Yuedan practiced until midnight. Shiniang and her husband left after Yang had roughly learned the piece.

Yang Yuedan played hard without taking his eyes off the musical instrument. Suddenly he understood the secret and could not help dancing. He raised his head and found the maid still standing by the candle. He asked, "Why haven't you gone?" The maid said with a smile, "Shiniang has told me to close the door and remove the candle after you go to sleep." Yang Yuedan took a close look at the beautiful maid and his heart jumped. The maid smiled back at him. Yang became aroused and hugged her. The maid said, "Don't behave like this. It's four o'clock in the morning. The master will get up soon. If we want, we can be together tomorrow evening." While the two embraced each other, Yan Haiyu called out, "Fendie." The maid was startled and said, "Sorry!" She hurried out. Yang Yuedan followed her and heard Yan Haiyu saying, "I said a long time ago this maid is no good. She still maintains human desires, but you wanted to keep her. She should be punished by being hanged three hundred times." Shiniang said, "Once her sexual desire has been aroused, it is difficult for us to continue to employ her. We had better ask her to leave." Yang Yuedan felt ashamed and frightened. He returned to his bedroom to sleep. When day broke, a boy servant came to help him with his washing. Fendie had disappeared, Yang Yuedan felt uneasy and was afraid that he would be blamed and driven away. Soon Yan Haiyu and Shiniang came to see him. They did not act differently towards him, and said they wished to hear how well he could play. After he had played a piece for them, Shiniang said, "You're not perfect, but you're nearly there." Yang Yuedan wanted to learn more from them. Yan Haiyu taught him to play another piece. It took him three days to learn how to play this difficult one. Yan Haiyu said, "You have played quite well. You need more practice. Soon you will be able to play this piece, then you will be able to play any other piece."

Yang Yuedan missed his home very much and said to Shiniang, "I am happy to stay here, especially with your help, Aunt, but my family must miss me. There is a distance of 1,500 kilometers separating me from my home. I don't know when I will return." Shiniang said, "It is not hard. Your old boat is still here. I could help you. Since you still haven't married, I have sent Fendie to your home to wait for you." She presented him with a musical instrument and some medicine, saying, "The medicine is for your grandma. It can cure her disease and also prolong her life." She saw him off at the shore. Yang Yuedan tried to look for the oars. Shiniang said, "They are unnecessary." She took off her skirt and tied it as a sail for the boat. Yang Yuedan was afraid that he would lose his direction. Shiniang told him, "Don't worry. Let the boat sail itself." Shiniang stepped back to the shore. Yang Yuedan was gripped by a sudden sadness. Before he said goodbye, the wind started blowing so hard that the boat quickly left the shore. Food had been set in the boat, but it was only enough for one day. He thought Shiniang was tight-fisted. He did not dare eat much as he feared that he would go hungry later. But when he finished one cake, he no longer felt hungry. The sun was setting and he regretted that he had not brought along some candles. Suddenly he caught sight of some houses. Already he had reached Qiongzhou. He was very glad. The boat reached shore, and he used the sail to wrap up the cakes to take home.

When he entered his home, all the family members were happy and very surprised. He had been away from home for sixteen years. He realized that he had met an immoral. His grandma was old and sick. Yang Yuedan gave her some medicine and she recovered very quickly. Everybody questioned him about his travels He told them what he had seen. The grandma said with tears, "It is your aunt." The grandma had a youngest daughter named Shiniang. She was married to Yan. The son-in-law at the age of sixteen never returned from a trip into the mountains. Shiniang waited until she reached the age of twenty and suddenly died one day. She had been buried for more than thirty years. After hearing what Yang Yuedan said, everybody suspected that Shiniang did not die. Yang Yuedan took out the skirt, which they recognized as the one she had worn when she was at home. He shared the cakes with everybody. They each only had one piece and for the entire day their hunger was gone. Also, they felt much stronger. Grandma asked the others to open Shiniang's tomb, which they found was empty.

Yang Yuedan had been engaged to the daughter of Mr. Wu

but they had not officially married. The girl married another man when Yang did not return for several years. Everybody believed what Shiniang had said and waited for Fendie to arrive, but there was no news for over a year. They had to make another arrangement. Scholar Qian in Lingao County had a daughter named Hesheng, who was famous for her beauty. She was sixteen years old and her three would-be husbands had all died before the wedding day. Yang sent a go-between to propose the marriage and selected a lucky day for the wedding. When the bride arrived, Yang Yuedan recognized her as Fendie. He asked her about the past but she did not remember at all. The day Fendie was driven out was the day Hesheng was born.

Whenever Yang Yuedan played the piece of music "The Birth of the Immortal," Fendie would always hold her jaw listening in deep thought, as if she somehow understood its true meaning.

TALE 51

The Death of Li Tansi

Li Tansi, a native of Changshan County, Shandong, was a student of the Imperial College. An old lady in his village knew how to serve in Hell through working for the people on the earth. She said to others, "Tonight I carried Tansi with another person to replace him in Bojiazhuang, Zichuan County. His body was so heavy that I was almost pressed to death."

At that time, Li Tansi was drinking with his guests happily. Everybody thought that what the old lady had said was nonsense. At night, Li Tansi died without any cause. After daybreak, someone checked, and just as the old lady had said, the family had a new baby girl.

TALE 52

Two Widows

In Taiyuan County, Shanxi, two widows, a woman and her daughter-in-law, lived together. The mother-in-law was middle-aged and lived a life of ill-repute. Often, a rascal from the village came to spend the night with her. The daughter-in-law looked down upon her and she often tried to stop the man from staying. The woman felt ashamed and made excuses to drive her out. The daughter-in-law, however, refused to go. The woman became frustrated and filed a false suit against her daughter-in-law.

The county official asked for the name of the person who maintained an illicit relationship with one of the two widows. The woman said, "That man comes and goes at night. I don't know who he is. You will know if you check with my daughter-in-law." The daughter-in-law was asked to testify in court and she knew the name of the man, but she insisted it was her mother-in-law who was visited by the man at night. In the end, both women had accused the other of having an illicit affair. Then the man was summoned. He said he had nothing to do with either woman. "They don't get along well, and are trying to involve me in their petty squabbles." The county official said, "There are over one hundred people in the village. Why would they single out you?" The official ordered the man tortured by the bailiffs. Trying to avoid the beating, the man begged the court's forgiveness and claimed he had been having an affair with the eighteen-year-old daughter-in-law. The county official had the young woman shackled. Still she professed her innocence. She was finally driven out. The daughter-in-law reported the case to the prefectural court where, as in the county court, there was no immediate solution.

Sun Liu, a scholar from Zichuan, was sent to Linjin County to serve as the magistrate of the county. He was regarded as capable in handling difficult cases, so the prefectural court asked him to solve this case. Mr. Sun questioned the three suspects and had all three jailed. Then he asked his people to prepare some bricks, stones, knives and other tools for use the next day. People did not understand what he was up to and asked him, "If you want to lock them away, we have enough shackles. What use do these tools have for this case?" Even though they were not given an answer, they obeyed the orders and prepared the articles.

The next day Mr. Sun checked whether the tools he asked for were ready and ordered his people to put them in the hall. He questioned the accused one by one. He said to the two women, "It is unnecessary to do any further investigating in this case. The woman has not been identified, but the man has been singled out. Both of you are not guilty, for you are good and honest people, only having been seduced by the man, so the man is guilty. Now there are tools in the hall, you can use them to kill the man." The two women were reluctant and afraid that they would be sentenced to death themselves if they killed the man. Mr. Sun said, "You don't have to worry. I'll take the responsibility." The two women stood up and began to stone the man. The daughter-in-law used a huge stone, as she had a strong hatred for this man. But the mother-in-law only used small stones to strike his legs and back. The magistrate ordered them to use knives. The daughter-in-law used the knife to stab him in the chest, while the mother-in-law was reluctant to draw blood. The magistrate stopped both of them and said, "I know which woman had an affair with the man." He ordered his people to torture the mother-in-law, and soon she confessed. The man was hanged thirty times and the case was finally concluded.

TALE 53
Wife and Concubine

Hong Daye was from Jingdu. His wife, Zhu, was a real beauty. The couple seemed to love each other dearly.

Later, Hong Daye took his maid Baodai as his concubine. Although Baodai was not as beautiful as Zhu, Daye loved her and pampered her more than he did his wife. His wife thus grew angry and the couple quarreled bitterly. From that point on, Hong Daye became all the more distant to his wife and closer to his concubine, although he no longer dared to openly sleep in his concubine's room.

The Hongs moved to a new neighborhood and lived next door to a silk businessman whose family name was Di. One day, Di's wife, Hengniang, visited Zhu. Hengniang was in her thirties, with rather ordinary features, and very talkative. Immediately, Zhu found herself enjoying her company. When Zhu visited Hengniang at her home the next day, she found there was also a concubine at the Dis' home. She was a little over twenty and very pretty. After living next door to the Dis for six months, Zhu had heard no complaint from Hengniang. Mr. Di was very much in love with Hengniang and the concubine was a wife only in name.

So one day, Zhu asked Hengniang, "I used to believe that men loved concubines because of what they were. How did you manage it? Please be my teacher and tell me." Hengniang said, "It's you who pulled yourself away from your husband, and yet you complain about men! You quarreled with him, always giving him a dressing down. You were driving him towards his concubine. You were drifting further and further away from him. What you should do for the moment is this, If he comes to you, refuse him. A month later, I'll tell you what to do next." Zhu went home, doing everything to make the concubine look more beautiful and forcing her to keep her husband company during the night. When she and her husband ate together, Zhu would ask the concubine to join them. Whenever Hong Daye wanted to be intimate with Zhu, Zhu refused him so he would have to seek comfort from the concubine. People all praised her as generous and kind.

A month later, Zhu went to see Hengniang again. Hengniang told her, "Go back and change into more shabby clothes. Don't wear any make-up. Wear old shoes. Work at home as if you are one of the maids. Come back again in a month." Zhu went home and did what she was told. Hong Daye took pity on her and told Baodai, the concubine, to help her with her chores. Zhu refused her help.

Another month passed and Zhu went to see Hengniang, who said, "The day after tomorrow is the Spring Outing Festival. I'll take you out. Put on your best clothes and come to me early in the morning." Zhu agreed. On that day, Zhu carefully did her make-up and followed all of Hengniang's instructions. When Hengniang saw her, she was satisfied, only changing Zhu's hairdo so that she looked all the more attractive. Hengniang also redid Zhu's robe to make it more fitting. She took out a pair of shoes that made Zhu's feet more beautiful. That evening, before Zhu went home, Heng-niang also offered Zhu some wine, saying, "Go home and let your husband see you for just a moment. Then shut up your door and sleep. If he comes and knocks at your door, don't open it. Accept him only after he pleads with you three times. Be mean with your tongue, hands and feet when you are together. Return again in two weeks' time." Zhu returned home and let her husband witness her radiant beauty. Hong Daye narrowed his eyes and examined her closely. He seemed happier than he had for some time. Zhu talked a little about her outing, put her hand under her chin as if she were tired. It was not quite dark yet, but she went her room to sleep, shutting her door behind her. A moment later, as expected, Hong Daye came and knocked on the door, but Zhu refused to open it. The next evening, the husband came again and once more was shut out. On the third day, the husband asked his wife why he was always kept out. Zhu said, "I'm accustomed to sleeping alone and do not want to be disturbed." Before sunset that evening, Hong Daye came into Zhu's room, refusing to leave. When they finally were in bed, they were like newly-weds enjoying their honeymoon. When it was over, the husband suggested they do this the following evening. Zhu would not agree, suggesting they go to bed together only once every three days.

Two weeks later, Zhu visited Hengniang, who whispered to her, "From now on, you can have your husband all to yourself. Though you're beautiful, you're not very charming. If you combine a little charm with your natural beauty, you will be unmatched." So Hengniang taught her how to cast eyes at men, telling her, "Your trouble is with your eyes." She also taught her to smile and said, "You're not doing it right. There's something wrong with the left part of your face." She patiently taught Zhu how to charm a man with her eyes and her coy smile. Having studied long and hard under Hengniang, Zhu felt much more confident. Hengniang told her, "Go home and practice in front of a mirror. Success in the wedding bed is something I cannot teach you. You must be flexible, make him happy."

At home, Zhu did as she was taught. Hong Daye was extremely happy and totally captivated by her. His only fear was being rejected by Zhu. Before the sun had set each evening, he was already busy charming and teasing his wife, not leaving her room for one single step. She found it impossible to keep him out of her room now. Zhu was kinder to Baodai, inviting her to join her and her husband for meals. To Daye, Baodai became more and more ugly. He would send her away before the meal was finished. Zhu trapped Daye in Baodai's room and locked the door from outside, but Daye would not even touch Baodai. In the end, Baodai felt insulted and began to speak ill of Daye, which only made Daye more irritated with her. In fact, now he spoke to her primarily through the cracks of whips and switches. Enraged, Baodai stopped worrying about appearances, wearing dirty clothes and shoes and keeping her hair like a heap of grass.

One day, Hengniang asked Zhu, "Did my method work?" Zhu told her, "It has worked beautifully. I have done what you taught me, but I still don't understand the principles. Why did you ask me to let my husband indulge himself in the first place?" Hengniang explained, "Don't you know men love what is new. They love concubines not necessarily because they are beautiful. They love them because they are new, and men like the rare opportunities of having another love. Let them enjoy their concubines to their hearts' content. There is always the time when they are tired of the concubine, no matter how good she is!" Zhu went on asking, "Then why did you tell me first not to wear make-up and to look shabby and later you want me to wear make-up and look attractive?" Hengniang told her, "If you leave something aside without looking at it, soon it will appear as if new. When men suddenly see women with make-up, they seem to have caught their new love. It's like a hungry man suddenly seeing delicious food in front of him, ordinary food immediately becomes tasteless. What you do at this time is not to let your man have you easily. In comparison, Baodai is old and ordinary while you're new. He can easily have her but you are hard to get. This is the method to replace the concubine with the original wife." Zhu was very happy to be told all this and the two women became bosom friends.

One day several years later, Hengniang suddenly said to Zhu, "We've been very close to each other and now there's something I should let you know. I did not tell you before because I was afraid you might be suspicious. Now I'm leaving and I have to let you know the truth, I'm a fox spirit. My mother died when I was very young and my step-mother sold me to Jingdu. My husband was very kind to me and so I could not leave him. I've stayed on until today. But my father will become an immortal tomorrow, and I have to pay him a visit. I won't be able to come back." Zhu held Hengniang's hand, sobbing. The next day, the Dis were in great turmoil as Hengniang suddenly disappeared.

TALE 54

Magistrate and the King

G overnor of Hunan dispatched a county magistrate to transport six hundred thousand ounces of silver to the capital.

While on the road, the magistrate encountered a heavy storm of rain, which delayed him that night. He was forced to take refuge in an old temple but, when morning came, he was horrified to find that the treasure had disappeared.

He returned to report to the Governor, who refused to believe what the magistrate had to him. After that, the magistrate got back to the temple where he met a blind man. The blind man told him to travel with him to a large city with a huge population.

They travelled for five days and finally reached the city. When they reached a place, the blind man cried "Stop!" and, pointing to a lofty door facing the west, he told the magistrate to knock and make what inquiries were necessary. The blind man then bowed and took his leave.

The magistrate knocked that door, but the master of that house was not at home. One day, he chanced to stroll away to the back of the building, and found a beautiful garden with dense avenues of trees.

There he met a man. The man led the magistrate inside; where the magistrate was shown a king, who wore a crown decorated with pearls, and an embroidered gown. He sat facing the south.

The magistrate prostrated himself on the ground and the King asked him if he was put in charge of transporting silvers to the capital.

The magistrate said yes and the king said, "The money is all here; it's a mere trifle, but I have no objection to receive it as a present from the Governor."

When the magistrate told the king he would be punished if he went back without completing his mission, the king said put a thick letter into his hands acknowledging the receipt of the gifts from the Governor.

TALE   55

Marrying a Nun

Chen Yu in Hubei was a good scholar and a handsome young man. When he was a boy, a physiognomist had predicted that he would marry a Taoist nun, but his parents regarded it only as a joke, and made several attempts to get him a wife.

One day, he paid a visit to his maternal grandmother in Huanggang, and was told there were some very pretty nuns living in a local temple which was a few miles from his grandmother's house.

While in the temple, he came up to a nun named Yunchi, the youngest girl there. She was so pretty that Chen could not keep his eyes off her. This made her blush very much, and she bent her head down.

When he attended a tea party, there, the nuns told him their names, Bai Yunshen, thirty odd years of age; Sheng Yunmian, twenty; and Liang Yuntong, twenty-four. Yunchi did not reappear, and others said she was afraid of strangers.

Disappointed as he was, Chen took his leave.

"If you want to see Yunchi you had better come again tomorrow," said Bai.

On the following day, Chen went there again, but, to his disappointment, all the nuns were there except Yunchi.

Chen was then invited to stay for dinner with them. Bai prepared food for Chen herself. Chen asked about Yunchi and Bai and other girls said Yunchi would come directly.

Chen agreed to remain. Wine was freely served until at last Chen said he was so tipsy he couldn't take any more, but Chen was told Yunchi would not appear. Hearing this, Chen went off in a huff, without saying goodbye to people there.

In the small hours, however, Chen went back to the temple as he could not forget Yunchi. He was taken to a courtyard, but he was told Yunchi had locked herself in.

Yunchi finally showed up and told Chen, "They all make me a bait to entice you. I do not wish to remain a nun, and if I could only meet with a gentleman like you, I would be a handmaid to him all the days of my life."

After this he always had Yunchi in his mind, and wanted very much to get another interview with her, but he was told his father was dangerously ill, and promptly set off on his way home. His father died. His mother insisted on his taking a wife; and he then told her that when he was with his grandmother at Huanggang, an arrangement had been made that he was to marry a Yunchi. His mother consented to this.

When he went back to the temple, however, Chen found there was only one old priestess employed in cooking her food there. She told Chen Yunchi was living in the northern quarter of the city. When he rushed there, he was told Yunchi had left.

Months later, Chen 'smother came. She went away to the Lily Hill to fulfil a vow she had made, and remained all night at an inn at the foot of the hill. That evening the landlord knocked at her door and ushered in a young priestess to share the room. The girl said her name was Yunchi.

Early in the morning Chen's mother left where she stayed overnight with Yunchi.

Upon home, she told Chen, "How will you face your relations with a nun for a wife?"

Chen made no reply. Shortly afterwards, when he went for his imperial examination, he presented himself at the address Yunchi gave him before. However, the young lady was found she had gone away half a month before.

Chen returned home and fell ill when his grandmother died and his mother set off to assist at her funeral. On her way back she missed the right road and reached the house of one named Ching, who turned out to be a cousin of hers.

She was invited to go in, and there she saw a young girl of about eighteen sitting in the parlour, and as great a beauty as she had ever set eyes on.

Chen's mother was always trying to make a good match for her son, and she asked who the young lady was.

She was told the girl was from the Wang family.

Chen 's mother and Miss Wang got on so extremely well together that they were already on the terms of mother and daughter. Miss Wang was invited to accompany her home, and she readily accepted.

Through talks, Miss Wang told her she was Yunchi.

"Is your name Yunchi?" said Chen in great astonishment. When the young lady asked him how he knew it, he told her the whole story.

"My real name is Wang," replied the young lady, "but the old Abbess, being very fond of me, made me take her own name."

Chen 's mother was overjoyed at all this, and an auspicious day was immediately fixed for the celebration of their marriage.

TALE 56

Ta Nan Works to Search His Father

Xi Changlie in Chengtu man had a wife and concubine named Ho Zhaojung. As his wife was critically ill, he took a second named Shen.

Shortly afterwards Ho gave birth to a son named Ta Nan. As Xi was out of the town for business purpose and had not returned, the second wife Shen turned them out of the house, making them a daily allowance of food.

When Ta Nan had become a big boy, his mother didn't ask for an increase of victuals. Instead, she worked hard to earn a little money by spinning. Seeing all children at his age go to school and learn to read, Ta Nan told his mother he wanted to go too.

She sent him to a private school for a few days' probation, but Ta Nan proved to be so clever that he soon beat the other boys. The school master was so pleased that he offered to teach him for nothing. His mother sent him regularly, and by the end of three years he had a first-rate knowledge of the Sacred Books.

One day he came home and asked his mother, asking her about his father. His mother could say nothing but told him,

"Whenever you pass the temple of the God of War on your way to school, you should go in and pray, that would make you grow faster."

Nan believed her mother was right and did according to her instructions.

One day, Ta Nan did not come home as usual, and his mother rushed to the school, where she didn't find him.

Where was Ta Nan then? In the morning, when he left the house, he followed the road without knowing whither he was going, until he met a man who was on his way to Guizhou, and said his name was Qian. Ta Nan went along with him.

When they arrived at Guizhou they dined together. Qian put some drug in Ta Nan's food which soon reduced him to a state of unconsciousness. Qian then carried him off to a temple. He told the abbot there Ta Nan was his son, but he had no money to continue his journey. The abbot bought Ta Nam and went away with the money.

When Ta Nam woke up, the abbot allowed him to leave. On his way back home, Ta Nan met gentleman named Qiang from Luzhou who took him to his own home at Luzhou.

While in Luzhou, Ta Nan asked everybody he met for news of his father, until one day he was told that there was a man named Xi among the Fujian traders.

Ta Nan then set off for Fujian and met a man named Chen, and continued to search for his father. Finally, he succeeded in finding his beloved son.

During the period of three or four years, his mother, Ho, had lived alone until the wife, Shen, wishing to reduce the expenses, tried to persuade her to find another husband. Ho was now able to support herself, she categorically refused to do so.

Tan Nan's father, Xi, who used to be a scholar by career,

had gone into business. When he knew his son had gone forth in search of his father, he asked all people he knew to keep a look-out for Ta Nan, and, at the same time, raising Ho from the status of concubine to that of wife.

As to Shen, after she had driven Xi away, she took two fresh husbands. Xi himself, letting bygones be bygones, gave orders that Shen should be called madam by all alike.

TALE 57

Stone from The Heaven

One day, in Shuntian, a man was fishing in the river, something caught his net. He brought up a stone about a foot in diameter, beautifully carved on all sides to resemble clustering hills and peaks. He was quite as pleased with this as if he had found some precious stone; and having had an elegant sandal-wood stand made for it, he set his prize upon the table.

This took place in Shuntian and the man was Xing Yunfei. He was an amateur mineralogist who would pay any price for a good specimen.

One day, a personage came and begged to see the stone. He examined it carefully and immediately handed it over to his servant. At the same time, he and his servant whipped their horses and rode away.

When that person and his servant rant to a bridge, they stopped running to have a rest. All of a sudden, the stone in the hand of the servant slipped and fell into the water. His master hired several divers, who were quite unable to find it.

He was a wealthy man and published a notice of reward. As

a result, many were tempted to seek for the stone. None of them succeeded in this regard.

Xing got the news and came too. Taking off his clothes, he quickly jumped in and brought the stone out, together with the sandal-wood stand which was still with it. He carried it off home, and put it in his inner room.

One day, an old man knocked at the door and asked to be allowed to see the stone. When the old man saw it, he said, "I lost it many months since. How does it come to be here? I pray you now restore it to me."

The old man said there were ninety-two grottoes, and the largest had five words, reading, "A stone from The Heaven above."

Xing realized that he must be a superhuman.

"Of course it is yours," replied Xing.

The old man then said, "This stone can choose its own master. I had better take it away with me, and three years hence you shall have it again. If, however, you insist on keeping it, then your span of life will be shortened by three years. Are you willing?"

Xing said he was. When this was done, he turned to Xing and told him that the grottoes on that stone represented the years of his life.

More than a year after this, Xing had occasion to go away on business, and in the night a thief broke in and carried off the stone,

taking nothing else at all. When Xing came home, he was dreadfully grieved, and made all possible inquiries and efforts to get it back, but without the slightest result.

A year later, Xing visited a nearby temple and noticed a man selling stones there. He was excited to find that piece of stone there, and brought it back.

A high official next offered Xing one hundred ounces of silver for it, but Xing refused to sell it to him. This enraged the high official, who then said he would work up a case against Xing. Xing was forced to sell it to him.

One night, he dreamed that a noble-looking personage said to him, "My name is Stone from The Heaven. I purposely quitted you for a year, but next year on the 20th of the eighth lunar month, at dawn, come to the Haitai Gate and buy me back for two strings of cash."

Xing was overjoyed at this dream, and went to the Haitai Gate the next day, where he purchased it back from the servants of that high official for two strings of cash.

When Xing was eighty-nine, robbers broke into his house and made off with the stone, and his son tried in vain to secure their capture.

A few days afterwards, Xing and his son were travelling with their servants. Suddenly, two men rushed forth, and, looking up into the air, acknowledged their crime, "Mr. Xing, please don't torment us thus! We took the stone, and sold it for only four ounces of silver."

The two men were then taken before the magistrate, where they at once acknowledged their guilt. Asking what had become of the stone, they said they had sold it to a member of the magistrate's family.

The magistrate gave it to one of his servants and bade him

place it in the treasury. Thereupon the stone slipped out of the servant's hand and broke into a hundred pieces, to the great astonishment of all present. The magistrate now had the thieves bambooed and sent them away; but Xing's son picked up the broken pieces of the stone, and later buried them in his father's grave.

TALE 58
Dongting Lake Lady

A man named Lin took a boat on the Dongting Lake. He was on his way back home after having failed at the imperial examination, when suddenly strains of music and singing were heard.

Lin was sleeping on the deck and the boatman failed to rouse him. Then a person came and lifted him up, letting him drop again on to the deck, where he was allowed to remain in the same drunken sleep as before.

The deafening ding of musical instruments playing partially woke up Ling. Smelling a delicious odor of perfumes filling the air around him, he opened his eyes and saw that the boat was crowded with beautiful girls. Knowing that something strange was happening, Lin pretended to be fast asleep.

A young maid stood quite close to Lin's head. Much smitten with this young lady wearing a Bair of stockings of a king-fisher's wing color, he took hold of her stocking with his teeth, causing her to fall forward flat on her face.

The king was very angry. He ordered his men to kill Lin.

Lin cried as he was being led away, "The king of the Dongting Lake was a mortal named Lin; your servant's name is Lin too. His Majesty was a disappointed candidate; your servant is one too. His Majesty met the Dragon Lady, and was made immortal; your servant has played a trick upon this girl, and he is to die. Why this inequality of fortunes?"

The king handed him writing materials, and ordered him to compose an ode upon a lady's head-dress. Lin said to the king. "It took ten years to complete the Songs of the Three Kingdoms; it may be known that the value of compositions depends more upon what the composer did."

The king laughed, and waited patiently from early morning till noon, when a copy of the verses was put into his hand. Lin then rose to take leave, and the king presented him with ten ounces of gold and a crystal square, and told him the crystal square would keep him off any danger he might encounter on the lake. Then the king and his men left.

When everything had been quiet for a long time, the boatmen emerged from the hold, and they continued their journey.

The wind was against the boat. All of a sudden, an iron cat appeared floating on the top of the water.

Lin sat in the middle of the boat, with the crystal square in his hand, and the mighty waves broke around without doing them any harm. Thus were they saved, and Lin returned home safely.

One day he paid a visit to the city of Wuchang, he heard of an old woman who wished to sell her daughter and said that anyone who had the fellow of a certain crystal square in her possession should be at liberty to take the girl.

Lin took his square with him and the old woman was delighted to see him. The young lady was about fifteen years of age, and possessed of surpassing beauty.

The old woman said her daughter had a crystal square and Lin said he had one too. So they compared their squares together, and there was not a fraction of difference between them, either in length or breadth. The girl rose to meet him with a smile, and then he was astonished to see that her stockings were the colour of a king-fisher's wing, and her appearance generally like that of the girl he had met on the Dongting lake.

The young lady laughed at this. Lin was highly pleased; and washing his hands, burnt incense, with his face towards the lake, as if it were the Imperial Court, and then they went home together.

Subsequently, when Lin had occasion to go to Wuchang, his wife asked to be allowed to avail herself of the opportunity to visit her parents; and when they reached the lake, she drew a hair-pin from her hair, and threw it into the water. Immediately a boat rose from the lake, and Lin's wife, stepping into it, vanished from sight like a bird on the wing. From then on, Lin's wife went home twice every year, and Lin soon became a very rich man.

TALE 59

A Man Becomes a Crow

Yu Jung, a native of Hunan, came from a poverty-stricken family. He was a scholar but he failed the imperial examination. On his way back home from the capital, he ran out of money.

Feeling uncomfortably hungry, he went to the Wuwang temple, where he poured out all his sorrows at the feet of the Buddha.

By the end of the worshipping, suddenly a man took him to the presence of King Wuwang, and then, falling on his knees, said, "Your Majesty, there is a vacancy among the black-robes; the appointment might be bestowed on this man."

The King assented, and Yu was given a black suit. When he had put on this suit, all of a sudden, he changed into a crow, and flew away.

He saw many fellow-crows, and joined them to settle on the masts of the boats and trees.

Two or three days passed, and the King provided him with a very elegant mate named Zhu Qing, who often warned him when he exposed himself too much in search of food.

One day a soldier on a military ship shot him in the breast with a cross-bow, but luckily Zhu Qing got away with him in her beak, and he was not captured. This enraged the other crows very much, and with their wings they flapped the water into big waves that all the boats were upset.

Zhu Qing took good care of her husband, but his wound was a severe one, and at dusk he was dead. All of a sudden, however, Yu woke up from a dream, and found he was lying in the temple.

He was told he had been dead for a few days but people in the temple found his body was not quite cold.

Three years afterwards he went to the capital to take part in the imperial examination. On his way back home, he visited that temple, where he prepared lots of food, and invited the crows to share the food, and prayed, "If Zhu Qing is among you, let her remain."

When the crows had had enough food, they all flew away.

This time, Yu passed the imperial examination. He made a special visit to the Wuwang Temple, and sacrificed a sheep as a feast for the crows and again he prayed as on the previous occasion.

That night he slept on the lake suddenly there came a beautiful young lady about twenty years of age!

"Hi, long time no see!" the lady said to Yu. "Remember Zhu Qing?"

Yu was overjoyed, and

inquired how she had come.

They then sat talking together like husband and wife reuniting after long absence.

Yu asked her to return with him on his way south, but Zhu Qing said she had to go west again.

Next morning Yu woke up to find he was in a big room where two candles burnt brightly. Zhuqing told him they were not on the boat, but in her home in Hanyang.

"My home is your home, so why need you go south?" she asked.

Yu then decided to stay with her and forgot all about going home.

Half a year later, Yu became anxious to return home, and asked Zhu Qing to go with him. However, Zhu Qing said, "I was not supposed to do that. As you already have a wife back at home, how would you put me? It is better for me to stop where I am, and thus you will have a second family."

She then prepared a parting feast for her husband, and he was on all fours that night. When it dawned next morning, he was on his own boat again.

A few months later, Yu went to visit Zhu Qing as she was to be in labor. The wife gave birth to a son, and they named him Hanchan which means "Born on the Han River".

A few months passed away, and then Zhu Qing sent her husband back in a boat to his old home. No sails or oars were used, but the boat sped along itself. After this Yu visited his wife frequently. Years later, Hanchan grew up to be a fine boy.

Yu's first wife had no children, so she was extremely anxious to see Hanchan. Zhu Qing agreed and the boy went back home with his father.

One day Hanchan was seriously ill, and died all of a sudden.

Yu's wife was overwhelmed with grief, and Yu then set off for Hanyang to see Zhu Qing. To his surprise, he found Hanchan there. When he asked his wife Zhu Qing about the why, Zhu Qing replied, "As I wanted my boy, I sent for him." When Yu said his first wife loved Hanchan, Zhu Qing said she had to wait until they had the second child.

Before long, Zhu Qing had twins, a boy and a girl. As it was inconvenient to travel to and from his old home three or four times a year, Yu moved with his family to Hanyang. The whole family lived in happiness and Hanchan passed the imperial examination at twelve.

TALE 60
Flower Nymphs

The camellias are twenty feet in height, the peonies are more than ten feet high, and many other precious flowers are in bloom… all this was part of the scene found in a temple at Mount Lao.

Nearby the temple was a house built by a man named Huang for the purpose of study. One day he saw from his window girl in the white who was wandering about amongst the flowers. When she went out to meet her, she was nowhere to be found.

One day, this girl dressed in white came together with a girl dressed in the red. Huang found the girl in the red was an exceedingly good-looking girl. When he got nearer to them, the girl in the red dress cried, "A man! There is a man here!"

Returning home he was absorbed in his own thoughts. Suddenly the girl he missed very much entered the room. She said to Huang, "I mistook you as a bad man. You frightened me to death. Now I know you are a great scholar."

The girl went on to say, "My name is Xiang Yu. I will sing you a song." She sang very well, and Huang grasped her hand and said,

"I pray you would come again whenever an opportunity may present itself."

From then on the girl frequently walked in to have a chat with Huang, but she would never bring her sister with her. Huang thought she should bring her here, but Xiang said her sister did not care for society in the same way that she herself did. She promised at the same time to try to persuade her to come some day in the near future.

One evening Xiang Yu arrived and told him they would have to part. Huang asked why but she would tell him nothing. This seemed very strange to Huang.

Next day, a gentleman visited the garden and dug up a white peony and carried it away. Huang now knew Xiang Yu was a flower nymph. When he was told the peony only lived a few days after being taken away, he wept bitterly, and composed an elegy in fifty stanzas, and he went daily to the pit from which his beloved white peony had been taken, and water the ground with his tears.

TALE 61
Tiger Guest

Kung was a young man who was going from his home town Minzhou to the capital for the imperial examination. When he reached Xinan, he stopped for a rest.

As he was having his lunch, a tall and noble-looking man walked in, and sat by the side of Kung. Apparently, he was a talkative person, and the two entered into conversation.

The man told Kung his name was Miao. They drank for a while before Kung continued his journey. When he had gone more than a few miles, his horse was taken ill, and lay down in the road. While he was waiting there with all his heavy baggage, Miao came. He lifted up the horse, carried it off on his back to the nearest inn, which was about seven miles distant.

Now Miao who believed him to be a superhuman treated him with good wine and food.

After the examination Kung joined some of his friends in a picnic at the Flowery Hill. Believed it or not, Miao appeared, carrying with him a large flagon and a ham. They then dined and wined to their hearts' content while composing lines one by one.

When one of them failed to give a line, he should be fined with a cup of wine, but he refused.

Miao could stand it, and roared like a dragon till the hills and valleys echoed again.

The others were angry at Miao's rudeness. Miao then threw himself on the ground in a passion, and with a roar changed into a tiger, immediately springing upon the company, and killing them all except Kung and another scholar named Qin. He then ran off roaring loudly.

Now this Qin had passed the imperial examination. Three years later, he revisited the Flowery Hill and encountered a man named Qi who was eaten up by Miao at the party.

Qi said, "I am now a slave of Miao's, and would not set free before he could kill someone else .This is why I am here to wait for the chance."

Qin went away from the forest immediately.

TALE 62

The Master Thief

Prince Wu often told his men any one of them would be given a generous award if he could perform something unusual. Responding to Prince Wu's generous offer, Baochu, one of his men, vowed to do so. He was as strong as a tiger and as agile as a monkey.

Prince Wu had a concubine, who was good at playing guitar. She was extremely careful of her guitar, and never allow others to see it unless on Prince's written order.

When Prince Wu entertained a guest with a feast one evening, his guest begged to be allowed to see this wonderful guitar, but the Prince said he could have a chance to see it on the following day. Baochu, who was standing by, said he could get it without troubling the Prince to write an order.

The Prince then told Baochu to do it. After scaling numerous walls, Baochu found himself near the lady's room. Lamps were burning brightly within and the doors were bolted and barred. He found it impossible to get in.

Baochu mewed several times like a cat. He then heard the

concubine to look after the situation. She had barely got outside the door when Baochu rushed in, and took away the guitar from a table before her.

The concubine shrieked out "thieves! thieves!"

The guards, seeing a man making off with the guitar, started in pursuit.

Arrows fell round Baochu like drops of rain, but he jumped onto the tree crests and disappeared. He returned to the banquest hall and presented the guitar to the entertained guest.

TALE 63

One Killed by a Millet Stalk

One fine day, some young men saw a beautiful lady, riding on a pony, come on their way. One of the young man said, "I can manage to make that girl laugh." A supper was at once staked by both sides on the result.

The said young man then ran to the front of the pony, and put a millet stalk around his neck while keeping shouting, "I'm going to die! I'm going to die!"

Well, the young lady did laugh as she passed by to the great amusement of the group of young men.

When she was already some distance away, these young men was surprised to see his tongue protruded, and his eyes were glazed - he was indeed dead.

Was it not strange that a man should be able to hang himself on a millet stalk?

TALE 64
Rat Wifet

Xi Shan from Gaomi used to travel around in Shandong. One day he was caught in a rain, and reached a place, where he was supposed to spend the night, very late in the night. He knocked at all the doors, but no one answered.

Suddenly a door flew open and an old man came out to invite Xi to enter.

"There are only three or four of us," said the hose. "My wife and daughter are fast asleep. We have some of leftover food..."

When Xi was having his dinner, the old man's daughter, A-Qin, got up. She was a slender and pretty-looking girl about seventeen. As Hsi Shan had an unmarried brother, he began to think directly that she would do for him.

The old man told Xi his name was Ku, and his children had all died save this one daughter. He also told Xi his daughter was not yet engaged.

By the end of the dinner, Xi told the old man he would never forget his kindness. "My younger brother, San Lang, is seventeen years old," he said. "May I hope that you will unite our families together, and not think it presumption on my part?"

Xi wanted to pay for the food, but the old man refused, saying, "I could hardly charge you anything for a single meal."

A month later, Xi Shan returned, but when he was getting closer to the village he met an old woman with a young lady, both dressed in deep mourning.

When the young lady turned round to look at him, she pulled the old woman's sleeve, and whispered something in her ear. The old woman stopped and said mournfully, "My husband has been killed by the falling of a wall. We are going to bury him today. There is no one at home but please wait here until we come back."

They returned in the dusk of the evening. The old woman told Xi that the people of the neighborhood were a bad lot, and that if A-Qin was to marry into his family, no time should be lost.

When they reached the house, the old woman lighted the lamp, and entertained Xi Shan, to good food.

Next day, they set off for Xi's home.

When they arrived at Xi Shan's home he related the whole story to his parents, who were very pleased at what had happened, and provided separate apartments for the old lady.

After choosing a lucky day, A-Qin was married to San Lang.

In four years later, one day Xi Shan happened to pass a night with the people who lived next door to the house where he had met A-Qin. After telling them the story of his having had nowhere to sleep, and taking refuge with the old man and woman, his host said to him, "You must make a mistake, Sir; the house you allude to belongs to my uncle, but was abandoned three years ago in consequence of its being haunted. It has now been uninhabited for a long time. What old man and woman can have entertained you there?"

From then on, Xi Shan could not dismiss the subject from

his thoughts.

One night A-Qin told San Lang that her mother was not very well, so he needn't come to bid her good-night as usual.

In the morning mother and daughter had disappeared, and San Lang was greatly alarmed.

San Lang had a step-brother, named Lan. When travelling on business, he passed a night at the house of a relative named Lu. During the night, mixed sounds of rat bidding, weeping and lamentation proceeded from their next-door neighbors, but he did not inquire the reason of it.

On his way back he heard the same sounds, and then asked what the cause of such demonstrations was. Lu told him that a few years ago an old widow and her daughter had come there to live, and that the mother had died about a month previously, leaving her child quite alone in the world.

Lan inquired what her name was, and Lu said it was Ku. "It's my sister-in-law," cried Lan, in amazement, and at once proceeded to knock at the door of the house.

He called out, "Open the door, please." A-Qin immediately opened the door and asked him in, and recounted to him the whole story of her troubles.

Lan said her husband missed her very much, but A-Qin replied, "I came hither with my mother to hide because I was not regarded as a human being."

When Lan told San Lang all about this, San Lang travelled all night until he reached where A-Qin was. Husband and wife were overjoyed to meet again.

The two built a granary and in about a year the granary was full, and before very long San Lang was a rich man. A-Qin persuaded her husband's parents to come and live with them. After this there were no more supernatural manifestations.

TALE 65

The Arrival of the Son

Deng Chengde, a native of Kaifeng, Henan, went to study in Yanzhou. He stayed in a run-down temple, writing domicile books for a living. At the end of the year, the officials and regular employees went home, leaving him alone in the temple. Early one morning, a beautiful young lady came to the temple. She burned some incense and bowed before the Buddha and then left. The next day, she did the same. At night when Deng Chengde lit a light and was going out to the courtyard, the lady arrived again. Deng Chengde asked her, "Why do you come so early?" The lady answered, "During the daytime, there are too many people and it is very noisy. It is better to come in the night. I am afraid that I will interrupt your sleep if I come too early. I saw lights just now and thought that you must have risen. So I came in." Deng Chengde teased her, saying, "There is no one in the temple. Why don't you stay here so that you don't have to come and go." The lady smiled, "Well, if there is no one here, how about you? Are you a ghost?" Deng Chengde found her lovely. After she finished praying, he tried to make love with her. The lady said,

"How can you behave like this in front of the Buddha? You don't even have a proper house and you want to do that! It's just wishful thinking!" Deng Chengde simply went on begging her. The lady said, "A village about fifteen kilometers from here has six or seven children who need a teacher. You may go and look for Li Qianchuan and ask for the job. You can pretend that you have brought your family with you and ask him to find a room for you. I can do the cooking for you. That will be a way we can hide our actions." Deng Chengde was afraid that he would be found committing a crime. The lady said, "Don't worry. My name is Fang Wenshu. I have no relatives and often stay at my uncle's home. Who will know about us?" Deng Chengde was very happy. After leaving Fang Wenshu, he went to see Li Qianchuan. The plan worked. It was decided that he would bring his family members before the New Year. Deng Chengde told the news to Fang Wenshu, who said she would wait for him by the roadside. Deng Chengde borrowed a horse and bid farewell to his colleagues. Fang Wenshu was indeed waiting for him by the road. Deng got off the horse and let Fang ride it.

When they reached the school, the two were very happy. For six years, they lived as husband and wife. Fang gave birth to a baby boy. Deng Chengde was excited to have a son and named him Yansheng. Fang Wenshu remarked, "We are not really husband and wife and I was about to leave you, but now this little thing has come along." Deng Chengde said, "If we were lucky and had enough money, I was planning to take you to my hometown. Why do you say you wanted to leave me?" Fang Wenshu told him, "I thank you, but I can't bear to be frowned upon by your wife. It would be bad for the baby, too." Deng Chengde said that his wife would not be jealous, but Fang Wenshu kept silent to indicate her doubts. A month later, Deng Chengde resigned his job and planned to do business together with Li Qianchuan's son. He said to Fang Wenshu, "I don't think I can become wealthy through teaching. I want to do business so that I can go home one day." Fang Wenshu still kept silent. At night, she suddenly took her child in her arms and tried to leave. Deng Chengde asked her, "What are you going to do?" Fang said, "I want to leave." Deng Chengde got up from the bed and chased after them. Fang Wenshu disappeared before the door was even opened. He was frightened and realized that she was not an ordinary human being. Since Fang had disappeared suddenly, he dared not tell the others the truth, but only said that she had gone to her mother's home.

At the beginning when Deng Chengde left his home, he told his wife Loushi that he would come back by the end of the year. She had not heard from him for several years, and news had been passed around that he had died. Loushi's brother had no children and planned to let his sister remarry. Loushi reasoned that she should follow the rule of staying single for at least three years after her husband died and she worked hard, weaving cloth. One night when she was about to close the door, a lady carrying a child entered the house and said, "I am returning to my mother's home. I am told that you live here alone. May I lodge here tonight?" Loushi accepted her and found her very beautiful and in her twenties. They slept on the same bed and teased her child. The baby was as fat as a melon. Loushi sighed, "I have no child like this since I am a widower." The lady said, "I find looking after this child is unacceptably tiresome. Would you please adopt him as your son?" Loushi said, "Even if you really can part with him, I don't have any milk to feed him." The lady assured her, "It's not difficult. When the baby was just born, I was also worried that I had no milk for him. I took some medicine and I had milk. I still have some medicine left. I can give it to you." She put a package at the window. Loushi thought this strange, but thought it all in jest. However, when she awoke, the baby was with her, but the mother was gone. Loushi was frightened. In the morning, the baby started crying and Loushi had to take the medicine. After a while she had milk and fed the baby. The baby grew with each passing day and soon began learning to speak. Loushi loved him just as if he were her own son. Since that day, she decided not to remarry. During the day, however, she had to tend to the baby and had no time to earn money. Life became harder.

The lady arrived one day suddenly. Loushi was afraid that she would take the baby back and told her that she was guilty by leaving without saying anything and how hard it was for her to raise the baby. The lady smiled, "When you say it is hard for you to raise my son, do you think that will stop me from taking my child back?" She waved her hand at the baby, who cried and ran to Loushi. The lady said, "So the baby doesn't recognize his mother. This baby can't be bought even if you want to spend a hundred taels of silver. I wouldn't sell him to you even if you could afford the money." Loushi's face went red with worry. The lady said, "Don't worry. I have come for the baby's sake. After I left you, I realized you probably had no money to raise this child, so I have brought you a dozen taels of silver." She handed over some silver to Loushi who declined, afraid the lady would use this as a ruse to take back the boy. The lady put the money on the bed and left the house. Loushi ran out of the door, but she was gone. Loushi suspected that the lady had an ill intention, but she was happy that the money could earn some interest to cover their living expenses.

Three years passed and Deng Chengde came back home after having made some money from his business. The couple was happy to see each other. Deng Chengde saw the baby and asked where he had come from. Loushi told him the story. Deng

Chengde asked, "What is his name?" His wife said, "His mother called him Yansheng." Deng Chengde said, "He is my son." He found that the date of his son's arrival was the date when he and Fang Wenshu parted. Deng Chengde told his wife how they met and then separated. The couple was happy and expected that Fang Wenshu would come again. She, however, never appeared.

TALE 66

The Beggar

Gao Yucheng, born into a rich family in Jincheng, was good at acupuncture. He treated people whether they were rich or poor.

A beggar came to the town lying on the roadside with a festering sore on his leg. The sore was so foul that people could not get near him. The locals were afraid that he would die so they fed him some food everyday. Gao Yucheng took pity on him and had him carried to his house, letting him stay in one of the rooms. His family members covered their noses, unable to stand the smell. Gao Yucheng treated him with acupuncture and gave him food everyday.

The beggar asked for dumplings one day, enraging the servants who shouted at him in disgust and called him ungrateful. After Gao Yucheng heard this, he asked his servants to give the man dumplings. Several days later, the beggar wanted to have meat and wine. One of the servants reported to the master, "This beggar is really absurd! It was hard for him to get a single meal in a day when he was lying by the roadside, but now he is not satisfied with three meals a day. When he was given dumplings, he asked for meat and wine. This kind of greedy man should be thrown out to the roadside." Gao Yucheng asked the servant how the beggar's sore was. The servant said, "The scab is coming off bit by bit. It seems that he can walk now, but he still pretends that he is suffering." Gao Yucheng said, "It won't cost much. Please give him some meat and wine. After he recovers, he will not hate us." The servant agreed, but actually did not give the food to the man. He chatted with his fellow servants and they laughed at their master, whom they thought was being very naive.

The next day, Gao Yucheng went to see the beggar himself. The beggar stood up on his crippled leg and expressed his gratitude to Gao, saying, "I was dying. Now with your help, I am recovering quickly. I am very grateful to you. Since I have just recovered, I am eager for a good meal." Gao Yucheng learned that his order was not obeyed and ordered the servant beaten. He ordered meat and wine for the beggar. The servant harbored resentment and set fire to the room where the beggar was staying. He deliberately shouted. Gao Yucheng got up and found the room had been reduced to ashes. He sighed and said, "The poor beggar must have died." He urged all the people to quench the fire, but the beggar was seen sleeping soundly in the midst of the fire, snoring loudly. He was awakened, and then asked with surprise, "Where is the house?" All the people present realized now that the beggar was no ordinary man.

Gao Yucheng respected the beggar all the more and let him stay in the guest room. Gao also provided him with clothes and stayed everyday with the beggar. When asked, the beggar said he was called Chen Jiu. Chen Jiu became healthier after several more days. He spoke with learning and charisma. He was good at playing chess. Gao Yucheng always lost when playing with him.

Meanwhile, Gao learned a few tricks from the beggar. Half a year passed, Chen Jiu did not leave. Gao Yucheng also felt that there was no fun without Chen Jiu. When Gao had guests, he would ask him to join the party. At dinners, when the die was cast, Chen Jiu always helped Gao and they got satisfactory numbers. Gao Yucheng was surprised and asked him to play some tricks, but Chen Jiu always said that he knew nothing about magic.

Chen Jiu said to Gao Yuchcng one day, "I want to leave now. You've been a great help. Today I shall invite you to a meal. Please do not bring any of the others along." Gao asked, "We have been getting along very well, why do you want to leave all of a sudden? And you do not have money, how can I let you be the host?" Chen Jiu insisted, "It won't cost much." Gao Yucheng asked where the dinner would be and was told that it would be right in Gao's own garden. It was in the middle of winter. Gao Yucheng was afraid it was too cold in the garden. Chen Jiu said, "It doesn't matter." Gao followed him to the garden and felt the air warming as if it was the beginning of spring. When they reached the pavilion, it was even warmer. There were many birds singing as if it was the end of the spring. The tables in the pavilion were inlaid with agate and jade. A crystal screen was so clear that shadows could be seen. Strangely, bushes and flowers could be seen in the screen. Also white birds were singing and jumping in the trees in the screen. When he tried to touch the screen with his hands, his fingers passed right through it. Gao Yucheng was startled.

When they sat down, a parrot cried, "Please serve tea." Soon a phoenix holding a red jade plate with two glass cups of tea in its beak appeared. After the tea was finished, the phoenix flew away. The parrot shouted again, "Please serve wine." Blue birds and yellow cranes flew out of the sun holding a wine pot and cups and placed them onto the table. In a short while, many birds set seafood and delicious dishes onto the table. There were tasty foods and delicious wines. Chen Jiu found Gao Yucheng was a great drinker and said, "You should use a bigger cup." The parrot soon called for a goblet. Out in the distance, lights flashed in the sky. A giant butterfly placed a large goblet on the table. The butterfly was even larger than a wild goose. The butterfly's wings were very elegant. Chen Jiu told the butterfly, "Please convince him to drink more." The butterfly suddenly became a beautiful lady wearing elegant embroidered gowns. She urged Gao Yucheng to drink more. Chen Jiu said again, "Please do something else." The lady started dancing and doing somersault without touching off any dust. She also sang a song, "There is laughter in the flowery bushes that touch the passer-by's face. Hairpins fell down and the walkers followed the butterfly to the east side of the fence." The song echoed in the air. Gao Yucheng felt very glad and drank together with the lady. Chen Jiu asked the lady to sit down and poured some wine for her. Gao Yucheng had drunk too much and he stood up to embrace the lady. Just then, he found that the lady had become an ugly woman with eye balls protruding forward and teeth extending outside of her mouth. She had black, wrinkled flesh that looked repulsed him. Gao Yucheng pulled away from her and trembled. Chen Jiu used chopsticks to beat the lady's sharp mouth and shouted, "Please go away immediately." The ugly woman turned into a butterfly and flew away.

Gao Yucheng calmed down

and said goodbye. The night scene was beautiful and he said to Chen Jiu, "Your delicious food was delivered from the sky. I think your home must be in the sky as well. Why don't you take me to have a visit?" Chen Jiu agreed. He grabbed Gao's hand and leapt into the air. Gao Yucheng felt that he was in the sky reaching a gate with an entrance like a well. The inside was as bright as daytime. The stone stairs were smooth and a tall tree was in blossom with red flowers. A lady under the tree was washing clothes. Gao Yucheng stared at her, forgetting to continue his steps. The lady became angry, saying, "Where does this crazy man come from? How can you be here?" She hit Gao Yucheng's back with a washing stick. Chen Jiu took him to another place and chastised him. Gao Yucheng awoke and felt ashamed for having been beaten by the woman. He found Chen Jiu standing on a cloud. Chen Jiu told him, "We shall be separated. Please remember and don't forget that your life won't be long. Tomorrow please hide yourself in the western mountains so that you can escape death." Gao Yucheng begged him to stay, but Chen Jiu left. Gao felt the cloud under him dropping slowly into his own garden. The scene in the garden was totally different from the scene of their banquet. He told the story to his wife and both of them wondered about the strange happenings. His back was red and swollen, but had a pleasant lingering fragrance.

Gao Yucheng got up very early the next morning. According to what Chen Jiu had instructed, he carried some dry food to the western mountains. It was very misty and hard to find the way. Gao was in a hurry and missed one step, falling into a deep misty hole. Fortunately he was not injured. After he woke he could only see the clouds and sighed, "The celestial being has asked me to run away from the disaster. But how can I escape from this hole." Later he saw some lights inside the hole. He walked farther into the cave and found three old men playing chess. They did not turn to Gao Yucheng even when they saw Gao watching them. After the game was finished, they put the chess pieces into a box and asked how Gao had come to this place. Gao told them how he had fallen into the hole and lost his way. One old man said, "This is not the human world and not a place for you to stay long. I can send you back." He took Gao to the bottom of the hole. Gao felt he was lifted by the clouds and reached the ground. He found it was autumn and the leaves were yellow and falling. He was surprised, saying, "I came in winter, how come it is deep autumn now?" He hurried home, frightening his wife and children. In fact, they were so terrified that they cried together. Gao Yucheng asked why. His wife said, "You have been away for three years and we thought you had died." Gao said, "It is very strange. I was only gone for a short time." He took out his dry food, which had become ashes. His wife said, "After you left, I dreamed two people in black with shining belts urged us to pay taxes and looked around in our house. They asked where you were. I shouted at them, "He is out. Even if you are sent by officials, how dare you come into a lady's bedroom?" The two men went out and said, "Strange." Gao Yucheng realized that he had met immortals while his wife had dreamed of ghosts.

Whenever Gao Yucheng entertained guests. He would put on the jacket hit by the stick. There was a nice smell that was neither like musk nor orchid. It smelled even more strongly when he perspired.

TALE 67

Castration

Ma Wanbao, a scholar in Dongchang, Shandong, was unrestrained. His wife Tianshi was also frivolous, but the couple loved each other dearly.

A lady lodged temporarily at their neighbor's house. The neighbor was an elderly widow. The lady said that she was badly treated by her parents-in-law and therefore was running away from home. She was good at sewing and did some house work for the old widow, who was happy to have her. She declared that she was able to do a form of massage that could cure women of difficult diseases. The old widow often came to visit Ma and his wife, telling them about the young woman and how capable she was. Tianshi listened without really paying much attention.

One day Mr. Ma stole a glance at the lady from a crack in the wall. The lady was about eighteen and very beautiful. Ma became infatuated with her. He formed a plan with his wife. They told the neighbor that Tianshi was sick, hoping to trick the young woman into visiting them. When the old widow arrived, she told Tianshi that the young lady was afraid to meet strange men. "Please ask your husband not to enter the room," she told Tianshi. But Tianshi made excuses, "Our house is small. My husband comes and goes. What can I do?" Then she had an idea, "I'll ask our uncle in Xicun to invite him to dinner. He will be gone all evening. It will be easy." The widow returned home to get the young woman, while the neighbor told her husband about her lies.

That evening, the old widow brought the young girl and asked Tianshi, "Is your husband gone?" Tianshi assured the widow that her husband would be gone all night. "Good!" the girl said. The elderly widow returned to her own home. Tianshi lit a candle and made the bed for the young girl. She let the Girl get into the bed first and then took off her clothes and put out the candle. Suddenly she jumped up. "I forgot to close the kitchen door. The dogs will steal our food if I don't close it." Getting out of bed, she went into the kitchen and let Ma sneak in. Quietly he walked through the dark and climbed into the bed with the young woman. "I have come to cure your disease," the young girl said. Ma kept silent.

The young lady massaged Ma's abdomen and stopped. She reached between his legs and found his penis. The girl was frightened and wanted to run away. She pulled back as if stung by a poisonous snake or scorpion. Ma told her to be still, and reached between her thighs. But he too found a penis where no penis should have been. It was Ma's turn to be shocked. He called for a candle. Tianshi thought her husband's little plot had failed, and she rushed in with a light. The "girl" knelt on the floor, begging for forgiveness. Tianshi was ashamed and frightened. She immediately walked out.

Ma questioned the young man and found out he was Wang Er'xi from Gucheng in Shandong. His elder brother was a disciple of Sang Chong of Lishi County, Shanxi. He had found this way of taking advantage of women by disguising himself as a woman and giving them a "massage". Ma asked him, "How many women have you raped?" Wang Er'xi replied, "I have only slept with sixteen, since I have just learned how to do this."

Ma thought that he should be punished with a life sentence and intended to bring charges against him at court, but he liked the man for his good looks. He decided to mete out his own punishment. He tied the boy's two arms behind him and cut off his penis. The man bled terribly and fainted. He regained consciousness after half an hour. Ma asked him to stay in bed and covered him with a quilt, "I shall treat you with medicine. After you recover, you will stay with me for the rest of your life. Otherwise if I sue you, you will definitely die." Wang Er'xi agreed. The next day, the old widow came. Ma lied to her, saying, "She turned out to be my niece Wang Er'jie. As she is unable to have any children, she was driven out of her home. We realized this after she told us her experience. She is not feeling well at the moment. We want to buy some medicine for her and talk with her husband about keeping her in our house to keep my wife's company." The old lady saw "Wang Er'jie" was pale and sat down beside the bed. "My private parts are swollen," the young boy told the widow. "I am afraid it is a bad sore." The old lady believed this and left.

Ma gave him some medicine and Wang soon recovered. At night they engaged in homosexual pleasures. During the daytime, Wang did the house work for Tianshi as if he were Ma's concubine.

Not long after, Sang Chong was caught and, together with seven disciples, was sentence to death. Only Wang Er'xi escaped death. Still, a warrant for his arrest was issued. The villagers suspected that "Wang Er'jie" was the escaped Wang Er'xi. Old women in the village gathered together to check if the girl was in fact a boy. They felt his private parts through his trousers. But as they felt no male organ, they believed he was truly a she. Wang Er'xi was grateful to Ma and lived with him for the rest of his life. After he died, Wang was buried together with the Ma family west of the town. His tomb can still be found.

TALE 68

The County Magistrate and an Aggressive Woman

The daughter of Mr. Weng from Linzi County, Shandong, was married to Mr. Li, a teacher at the Imperial College. Before their marriage, a fortune teller predicted that the woman would some day be punished by officials. Mr. Weng was first enraged by this and then could not help laughing out aloud, "It cannot be more absurd. Not only to say a girl from a gentleman's family like ours, who will never commit any offence, will be brought to court, but how can a teacher fail to protect his wife?"

Once Mr. Weng's daughter was married, she acted as a very aggressive woman whose swearing at her husband became a daily routine. Unable to put up with her any more, Mr. Li brought a charge against His wife in the court. The county magistrate, Mr. Shao, sent bailiffs to bring the woman to the court. Her father, Mr. Weng, was scared by the news and hurried to the court along with his sons and nephews, pleading to the county magistrate to drop the case. Mr. Shao refused the plea. Mr. Li, the husband, regretted what he had done and appealed to withdraw his charge. Mr. Shao, the magistrate, flew into a rage, "Who do you think you are, telling the court to try a case and then asking the court to drop it? I'm going to try the case anyway." When the woman was brought to the court, the magistrate asked her one or two questions and came to the conclusion, "She is really a bitch!" He then sentenced her to thirty beatings. When this was carried out, her back was a bloody mess.

The unofficial historian remarked, The magistrate must have had a strong resentment towards bad behaviors by women, otherwise why should he fly into such a rage. With such a strict official, however, there would not be any unreasonable and aggressive women in the county. So this incident must be recorded to make up the inadequacies of biographies of enlightened officials.

TALE 69
A Test of Loyalty

Scholar Dong from Xuzhou, Jiangsu, loved to play with swords and took pride in being a gallant man. One day he ran into a traveler on the way and they traveled together on donkey backs. Mr. Dong learned that the other traveler was from Liaoyang and his family name was Tong. Tong explained, "I've been away from home for twenty years and have just returned from overseas." Mr. Dong asked, "Since you have traveled so widely and known so many people, have you ever met any people with special skills?" The traveler replied, "What kind of special skills do you mean?" Mr. Dong told the traveler about his special interest in the art of fencing and his regret in having not met any people who really knew the art well enough to teach him. The traveler said, "People with special skills are easy to find, but only those loyal and honest can be taught the real skills." So Mr. Dong talked about how honest he was and pulled out his sword, pointing at it and using it to cut trees along the way, admiring the sharpness of the blade.

Traveler Tong touched his beard, smiled and asked to see

the sword. Mr. Dong gave it to him. After examining it for a while, Traveler Tong said, "This sword was made with melted armor and has long been soaked in sweat. It is but the cheapest kind. I don't understand the art of fencing, but I do have a sword, a very good one." He took out his sword, only lout a foot long, and began to use it to peel Mr. Dong's sword and cut it into small slivers. Mr. Dong's sword fell off like a cucumber being cut with a sharp knife. Mr. Dong was greatly surprised. He took his travel companion's short sword, examined it and touched it before he returned it. He invited the traveler to his house and asked the man to stay for two days so that he could learn fencing from him, but the traveler insisted that he knew nothing about the art. Mr. Dong then began to talk in great length about fencing and the traveler simply listened.

It grew late and suddenly noises were heard in the next compound where Dong's father lived. Mr. Dong was both surprised and suspicious of the noises. He leaned over at the wall and heard someone shouting, "Call your son out and let me kill him or I won't let you go!" Soon fighting was heard and someone began moaning. From the voice, he sensed it was his father. Mr. Dong picked up a sword and was ready to jump over, but was stopped by the traveler who said, "The robber asked for you and will try to get you. Since you have no other relatives, you should leave your will with your wife. I'll go and get your servants up." Mr. Dong agreed and went into the house, making his final arrangements with his wife, who cried, pulling at his clothes. Dong's determinations disappeared and the couple hid themselves upstairs, where they found arrows to protect themselves in case the robbers came in. Just then, they heard Traveler Tong laugh, "Thank goodness, the robbers are gone." Mr. Dong aimed his light at the traveler, who had totally disappeared. Next he saw his father going out to drink at his neighbor's house and all that was in the courtyard was a heap of ash from grass torches. He realized that the traveler was a person of unusual skills.

The unofficial historian remarked, Filial piety and loyalty are a man's strength. Since antiquity, did those who failed to give their lives to protecting their emperors or fathers ever have a moment of gallantry? But a moment of hesitation ended in a life-long mistake. In history, Xie Jin agreed with Fang Xiaoru that they would die for Emperor Jianwen if necessary, but did not carry out his promise. Who knew that when he went home after having enjoyed pleasures with Fang Xiaoru, his wife would cry again and again in fear of his death? In my county, a civil servant is often away from home and his wife thus maintained illicit relationship with a scoundrel. One day, the man came home and the scoundrel escaped from his wife's room. Suspicious, he pressed the issue with his wife who categorically denied having an affair with the man. Later he found on the bed something left by the scoundrel and next his wife knelt in front of him, begging for leniency. The civil servant was greatly enraged, threw a piece of rope at his wife and told her to hang herself. The woman begged for permission to dress before she died and the husband agreed. She entered the bedroom to dress up while he drank by himself in the sitting room, now and then urging her to hurry up. Later, his wife came out, fully dressed and said while kneeling down and sobbing, "Are you going to really be so hard as to send me to die?" Her final plea was only greeted with more swearing. His wife turned inside and when she was about to tighten the rope, the man threw the wine cup on the floor and shouted, "Come out now. I don't think people's talk of me will weigh me down." So the couple made up again. He in a way was also like Xie Jin whose story makes people laugh.

TALE 70

A Severe Punishment

Once there was a local man who was a vicious character. One morning after he got up, two men came over, dragged him to a butcher's and pushed him next to half a pig hanging on the rack. The man immediately felt as if he had become the other half of the dead pig, and the two men who brought him over quickly walked away. Very soon, the butcher began to cut the meat and sell it, and the man felt the pain of each cut. An old man who was his neighbor also came to buy meat. The butcher cut a piece, weighed it and had to cut a few more small pieces. And the cutting made him feel even more piercingly painful. It was not until the half pig was gone that the man was able to escape home. It was already nine o'clock when he made his way home and his family members thought he had just got out of bed. He told them his experience at the butcher's. They brought in the neighbor who had bought some meat, questioned him about the weight, and number of chunks, and the figures matched what the man had said. It is thus something unusual for a man to be punished by going through the experience of being cut up like a piece of meat.

TALE 71

Man Thrown down a Well

A young man named Tai, a native of Anching, was one day returning home tipsy. All of a sudden, he encountered a dead cousin of his named Chi. Still in his drunken state, he asked him where he was going.

"I am already a disembodied spirit," Chi said, "Don't you forget?"

Under the influence of liquor, Tai was not frightened, and inquired of Chi what he was doing in the netherworld.

"I am employed as scribe," said Chi.

"Then you must know all about our happiness and misfortunes to come," said Tai.

"Three days ago, I saw your name in the register."

Tai was dreadfully alarmed.

"It is now too late, but there may still be a chance of escape for you."

Tai implored his cousin to help him, but Chi had disappeared.

Tai returned home sorrowfully. He began to mend his ways

in daily behavior.

One day after that, Tai's next-door neighbor, who had long suspected Tai of trying to seduce his wife, inveigled Tai to inspect a dry well. All of a sudden, however, he pushed him down.

In the middle of the night he came round, and began to shout for help.

On the following day, the neighbor went to the well and threw down many stones. Tai took refuge in a cave at the side.

He felt hungry, and he passed his time in praying for help from Buddha. A sound was heard to tell him, "This was an old coal-mine. The proprietor organized the laborers and this angered a man named Lungfei, said to be secretary to the City God. He then directed water into the coal pit and, as a result, forty-three workmen were drowned here. Need help? Wear the shades of those men."

The souls of the 48 dead workers said to Tai, "If you some day return to the world above, I pray you fish up our decaying bones and bury them in some public tomb yards." Tai promised to do so.

Four years had passed by. During the period, Tai's wife married another husband. However, one found all of a sudden from the well cave Tai was not dead, and was promptly brought back home. Just in a day he woke up and told the family the whole story.

Tai was told his neighbor who pushed him in had beaten his own wife to death was sentenced to sit behind the bar for more than a year while the case was being investigated. When released he was a bag of bones.

Tai hired men to collect the bones of that forty-eight coal miners from the well, and put them in coffins and buried all together in one place.

TALE 72

The Virtuous Daughter-in-Law

Dacheng's father was a good scholar. He passed the imperial examination but died when Dacheng was still young and Dacheng's brother Ercheng was a mere boy.

Dacheng's wife Shanhu was a virtuous woman. Her mother-in-law was picky but Shanhu never complained. Dacheng was a very filial son. Because of his mother's unhappiness, he once beat his wife. However, his mother was often not satisfied, and hated her daughter-in-law more than ever. This forced Dacheng to blame Shanhu for every trifle that occurred. He even bade Shanhu begone.

When Shanhu was out of the house, she burst into tears, and drew a Bair of scissors and stabbed herself in the throat.

was therefore supported to the house of her husband's aunt, who was a widow living by herself.

In a few days Shanhu's wound was healed, and Dacheng asked his aunt to send her away. His aunt declined. Dacheng accused his wife of having failed in her duty towards his mother, but Shanhu made no answer, with tears trickling from her eyes. Dacheng was much touched by this, and went away without saying any more.

Before long his mother hurried off to the aunt's, and began abusing her roundly. This aunt said it was all the fault of her own bad temper, "The girl has already left you, and do you still claim to decide with whom she is to live?" This made Tacheng's mother furious, but she went off home abashed.

Shanhu herself was very much upset, and finally took up her abode with his mother-in-law's elder sister named Yu, over sixty of age. Yu's son had died, leaving his wife and child to his mother's care.

Yu was extremely fond of Shanhu, and said it was all her sister's horrid disposition.

Dacheng's mother had been endeavoring to get him another wife but the fame of her temper had spread so far and wide that no one would entertain her proposals. In four years Ercheng had grown up, and his wife was a young lady named Zang Ku, who was later found to be notorious in hot temper. Her mother-in-law could not stand this.

The mother-in-law seemed never to be able to please Zang Ku,k and the daughter-in-law even worked her mother-in-law like a slave, and Dacheng himself not ventured to interfere.

When Dacheng's mother told her sister all about this, her sister said Shanhu was a nice girl. "What a good daughter-in-law you have got, to be sure. What have you done to her?"

"I must have been as senseless as a statue not to have seen

what she was."

As a result, Shanhu returned to her husband. Unfortunately, Dacheng's mother soon died and Shanhu was so sad about this that she fused to take any nourishment.

Shen cried "My mother-in-law has died thus early. The Heaven will not allow me to retrieve my past errors."

Zang Ku had thirteen children, but none of them lived, forcing the couple to adopt one of Dacheng's. Dacheng and Shanhu lived to a good old age, and had three sons, two of whom passed the imperial examinations.

TALE 73

Zheng's Nightmare

When Fujian man named Zheng had passed his imperial examination, he celebrated his success together with other successors. At the party, they were told there was a very good astrologer living in the nearby temple. So they went to visit him.

These scholars put various kinds question to the astrologer.

"Have I any chance of ever wearing the dragon robes and the jade girdle?" asked Zheng jokingly.

The astrologer said seriously, "You would be a Secretary of State during twenty years of national tranquility."

Zheng was much pleased, and began to give himself greater airs than ever.

At noon, Zheng took a nap, when suddenly in walked two officials bearing a commission under the Great Seal appointing Zheng to the Grand Secretariat. Zheng u rushed off at once to pay his respects to the Emperor, who issued instructions that the promotion and dismissal of all officers below the third grade should be vested in Zheng alone. He was next presented with the dragon robes, the jade girdle, and a horse from the imperial stables.

When Zheng reached his own home, he found it had become a home with painted beams, carved pillars, and a general profusion of luxury and elegance.

As he was at the threshold of his gate, the responses of numberless attendants echoed through the place like thunder. He was served with costly food...

All the officials under him came to pay him visits and present him gifts. All day long he had nothing to do but find amusement as best he could.

When he went out in his sedan chair, a drunken man bumped against one of his tablet-bearers. Zheng had him seized and sent in to the county magistrate's yamen, where he was tortured to death.

Gradually his fellow-officials became estranged, and he offended the Emperor. And Zheng lost all he owned. He kept crying, crying loudly...

Suddenly, Zheng heard one of his companions call out, "Hello, there! you've got nightmare."

Zheng got up and rubbed his eyes, and his friends said, "You've taken a long nap. It's quite late in the day, and we're all very hungry."

TALE 74

Play Football on the Lake

Wang Shixiu, a native of Luzhou, was strong enough to pick up a stone mortar without much effort. He and his son were both good football players. When the father was close to forty years of age he was drowned while crossing a river.

Nine years later Wang was in Hunan, and his boat anchored in the Dongting lake. Watching the moon rising in the east, he enjoyed the rippling water himself on the deck.

Suddenly, five men emerged from out of the lake, ringing with them a large mat They spread the mat on the surface of the water about six yards square. Wine and food were then arranged upon it.

Three of them sat on the mat, while two others stood by. Of the three, one was dressed in yellow, the other two in white, and each wore a black turban. The attendants wore black serge dresses. Soon, they rose to pay football.

The ball was kicked up some ten feet in the air, and fell right in Wang's boat. Wang kicked it with all his might. Down it glided into the water, where it fizzed a moment and then went out.

"Well kicked indeed!" said the old man. "That's a favorite drop-kick of my own." At this, one of the two in white clothes began to abuse him, saying, "Go at once with the boy and bring back to us this practical joker, or your own back will have a taste of the stick."

Wang was not a bit afraid, and grasping a sword stood there in the middle of the boat. In a moment, the old man and boy arrived, also armed, and then Wang knew that the former was really his father, and called out to him at once, "Father, I am your son." The old man was greatly alarmed, but father and son forgot their troubles in the joy of meeting once again.

All this happened when that three men jumped on board the boat. Their faces were black as pitch, their eyes as big as pomegranates, and they at once proceeded to seize the old man.

Wang struggled hard with them, and seized his sword and cut off one of his adversaries' arms. The arm dropped down and that man in the yellow dress ran away. One of those in white rushed at Wang, and Wang immediately cut off his head...

Wang and his father were now anxious to get away, when suddenly a great mouth arose and blew forth a violent gust of wind, and in a moment the waves were surging so high that all the boats on the lake were tossing about.

Wang believed his father was a disembodied spirit, but the old man said, "I have never died. Nineteen of us drowned in the river, and we were all eaten by the fish-goblins except myself."

When Wang asked why, the father said, "I was saved because I could play foot-ball."

TALE   75

The Thunder God

Yo Yunhao and Xia Pingzhu were born and brought up in the same village. They studied from the same tutor, becoming best friends. Xia had acquired some reputation even at the early age of ten, and Xia helped his friend very much with his studies, so that Yo also made considerable progress. However, Xia became sickened and eventually died. His family was so poor they could not find money for his burial, whereupon Yo came forward and paid all expenses, besides taking care of his widow and children.

For economic purpose, he decided to do business. One day, when he was resting at an inn in Nanjing, he saw a great big fellow looking at him in a very melancholy mood. He looks he was hungry, and Yo pushed some food over towards him.

"For three years I haven't had such a meal," the man said to Yo. When asked where he lived, the replied, "I have no home." The two decided to travel together.

Next day when they were on the river, a great storm arose and capsized all their boats, Yo was thrown into the water, but the man bore Yo on his back to another boat. Yo thanked him for his effort to save his life. Given all the man had done just know, Yo began to regard the stranger as something more than human.

When the man wished to leave, Yo urged him to stay and the man finally agreed.

One day it was about to rain and thunder.

"Would you like to have a ramble among the clouds?" asked the man.

Yo jumped up in great alarm. He felt giddy as if he had been at sea. Above him were the stars, and this made him think he was dreaming. On raising his hand he discovered that the large stars were all tightly fixed; but he managed to pick a small one, which he concealed in his sleeve; and then, parting the clouds beneath him, he looked through and saw the sea glittering like silver below. Large cities appeared no bigger than beans.

Now Yo was thirty years of age, but without sons. After this dream his wife bore him a son, and they named him Xin meaning Star. He was extraordinarily clever, and at sixteen years of age passed the regional imperial examination.

TALE 76

The Talisman of a Gambler

A Taoist priest, named Han, lived at the Tianchi temple. He was so good at his black art that all regarded him as an Immortal.

A relative of mine was terribly given to gambling. He knew this priest. Once this relative met with a Buddhist priest from the Tianfo temple, and was addicted like himself to the vice of gambling.

When that man told Han he had lost his money, Han laughed and said, "That's what always overtakes the gambler, but you will break yourself of the habit, I will get your money back for you."

Han gave him a talismanic formula, written out on a piece of paper, to put in his girdle, bidding him only win back what he had lost, and not attempt to get a fraction more.

Believe it or not, he did win again, going on and on until the latter's good luck had brought him back all that he had previously lost.

TALE 77

Punishing the Husband

Qing Xing, a Wenteng man of some literary reputation, had a next-door neighbor, whose name was Chen. Their studios were separated only by a low wall.

One evening Chen was passing through a deserted place when he heard a young girl crying in the woods. He went over and found a girdle hanging from a branch. With tears in eyes, the girl said, "My mother has gone away and left me to my brother-in-law, but he's a scamp, and won't continue to take care of me."

Chen untied the girdle and offered to take her to his own home - an offer which she very gladly accepted.

When the girl and Chen reached Chen's home, the girl agreed to take up her residence with Ching, but after a few days, finding that a great number of his friends were constantly calling, she declared it was too noisy a place for her, and that she would only visit him in the evening. This she continued to do for a few days, telling him in reply to his inquiries that her home was not very far off.

One day, the girl said her father was a mandarin on the western frontier, and she was about to set out with her mother to join him. She begged him to make a formal request for their nuptials. However, Ching told himself that if he married her she would have to take her place in the family, and that would make his first wife jealous. He then decided to get rid of the girl.

When he finally had got rid of her, he set to work at once to get the house whitewashed and made generally clean, himself being on the tip-toe of expectation for the arrival of Miss A-Xia.

One day, at the festival of the Sea Spirits, he saw among the crowds of girls passing in and out one who very much resembled A-Xia. Ching moved towards her, following her as she threaded her way through the crowd as far as the temple gate, where he lost sight of her altogether, to his great mortification and regret.

Another six months passed away, when one day he met a young lady dressed in red, accompanied by an old man who was her servant, and riding on a black mule. Ching thought she might be A-Xia, but the old man said she was the second wife of a gentleman named Cheng. Ching was overwhelmed with rage, and cried out in a loud voice, "A-Xia, why did you break faith?"

"To be faithless to your wife is worse than being faithless to me," rejoined A-Xia. "If you behaved like that to her, how should I have been treated at your hands? Because of the fair

fame of your ancestors, and the honors gained by them, I was willing to ally myself with you; but now that you have discarded your wife, your thread of official advancement has been cut short in the realms below, and Mr. Chen is to take the place that should have been yours at the head of the examination list. As for myself, I am now part of the Cheng family..."

Ching hung his head and could make no reply, and A-Xia whipped up her mule and disappeared from his sight, leaving him to return home disconsolate.

At the forthcoming examination, everything turned out as she had predicted, Chen was at the top of the list, and he himself was thrown out. It was clear that his luck was gone.

At forty he had no wife, and was so poor that he was glad to pick up a meal where he could.

TALE 78

The Marriage Bond

Ma Tianjun lost his wife when he was only twenty, and was too poor to take another. One day when out hoeing in the fields, he met a nice-looking young lady walking towards him. She appeared to have lost her way.

That night, strange enough, the young lady visited Ma but her face was covered with fine hair, which made him suspect at once she was a fox spirit. Ma said to her, "If you really are one of those wonderful creatures, you'd better get me some money to relieve my poverty."

A few nights afterwards Ma asked her once more for the money, and then he drew from her sleeve two pieces of silver, each weighing about six ounces. Ma was very pleased and stored them away in a cupboard.

Some months after this, he took out these silver, but these were found to be of pewter. Ma was much alarmed.

A few months passed away, and then one day the young lady came and gave Ma three ounces of silver, saying, "You have often asked me for money, but in consequence of your weak luck I have always refrained from giving you any. Your marriage is at hand, and I here give you the cost of a wife, which you may also regard as a parting gift from me."

"What will she be like?" asked Ma.

The young lady said, "She will be possessed of surpassing beauty."

"I hardly expect that," said Ma. "Three ounces of silver will not be enough to get a wife."

When morning came, she departed, giving Ma a pinch of yellow powder, saying, "In case you are ill after we are separated, this will cure you."

Next day, a go-between did come, and Ma at once asked what the proposed bride was like. Four ounces of silver was fixed as the marriage present.

"A relative of mine lives in the same court, and just now I saw the young lady sitting in the hall. We have only got to pretend we are going to see my relative, and you will be able to get a glimpse of her."

Ma consented, and they accordingly passed through the hall, where he saw the young lady sitting down with her head bent forward while someone was scratching her back.

She seemed to be all that the go-between had said; but when they came to discuss the money, it appeared the young lady only wanted one or two ounces of silver, just to buy herself a few clothes, which Ma thought was a very small amount, and gave the go-between a present for her trouble, which just finished up the three ounces his fox friend had provided.

An auspicious day was chosen, and the young lady came over to his house.

However, she was not a beauty, but an ugly woman who was hump-backed and pigeon-breasted, and had a neck as short as a tortoise.

TALE 79

Cricket Fighting

During the reign of Emperor Xuande of the Ming dynasty, cricket fighting was very much in vogue at court, levies of crickets being exacted from the people as a tax.

On day, the magistrate of Huayin, wishing to make friends with the Governor, presented him with a cricket which, on being set to fight, displayed very remarkable powers; so much so that the Governor commanded the magistrate to supply him regularly with these insects. The latter, in his turn, ordered the beadles of his district

to provide him with crickets; and then it became a practice for people who had nothing else to do to catch and rear them for this purpose.

As a result, the price of crickets soared, and when the beadle's runners came to exact even a single one, it was enough to ruin several families.

When there was a call for crickets, a man named Cheng tried to find one for an official in charge of regional imperial examinations. He got one famed as the Champion but he tried to test it. So he went to th4e cricket market.

One young fellow there laughed heartily at Cheng's Champion. He produced his own and placed it side by side, to the great disadvantage of the Champion.

Cheng's countenance fell, and he no longer wished to back his cricket.

However, the young fellow urged him, and he thought that there was no use in rearing a feeble insect, and that he had better sacrifice it for a laugh; so they put them together in a bowl.

The little cricket lay quite still like a piece of wood, at which the young fellow roared again, and louder than ever when it did not move even though tickled with a pig's bristle.

By dint of tickling it was roused at last, and then it fell upon its adversary with such fury, that in a moment the young fellow's cricket would have been killed outright had not its master interfered and stopped the fight. The little cricket then stood up and chirped to Cheng as a sign of victory; and Cheng, overjoyed, was just talking over the battle with the young fellow when a cock caught sight of the insect, and ran up to eat it.

Cheng was in a great state of alarm; but the cock luckily missed its aim, and the cricket hopped away, its enemy pursuing at full speed but in vain.

The magistrate put it into a golden cage, and forwarded it to the palace, accompanied by some remarks on its performances; and when there, it was found that of all the splendid collection of the emperor, not one was worthy to be placed alongside of this one. It would dance in time to music, and thus became a great favorite, the emperor in return bestowing magnificent gifts of horses and silks upon the magistrate.

The magistrate did not forget whence he had obtained the cricket, and well rewarded Cheng by excusing him from the duties of beadle, and by instructing the Literary Chancellor to pass him for the regional examination.

TALE 80
Taking Revenge

Xiang Kao in Taiyuan was deeply attached to his half-brother Sheng. Sheng, however, was desperately enamored of a young lady named Po Su. Po Shu was also very fond of Sheng, but her mother demanded too much money for her daughter.

A rich young fellow named Zhuang proposed to buy her as a concubine, but Po Su refused to agree and wanted to marry Sheng.

Sheng's wife had just died and Po Su's mother informed him of the news. Sheng was delighted and made preparations to take her over to his own house.

Zhuang was angry about his. One day, Zhuang chanced to meet him out one day, and Sheng answered him back. Zhuang ordered his men to beat Zhuang well, leaving him lifeless on the ground.

Xiang ran out and found his brother lying dead upon the ground. Overcome with grief, he proceeded to the magistrate's, and accused Zhuang of murder; but the latter bribed so heavily that nothing came of the accusation.

This worked Xiang to frenzy, and he determined to assassinate Zhuang on the high road; with which intent he daily concealed himself, with a sharp knife about him, among the bushes on the hill-side, waiting for Zhuang to pass.

This plan of his became known far and wide, and accordingly Zhuang never went out except with a strong bodyguard, besides which he engaged at a high price the services of a very skilful archer, named Qiao Tong, so that Xiang had no means of carrying out his intention.

However, he continued to lie in wait day after day, and on one occasion it began to rain heavily, and in a short time Xiang was wet through to the skin. Then the wind got up, and a hailstorm followed, and by-and-by Xiang was quite numbed with the cold.

On the top of the hill there was a small temple wherein lived a Taoist priest. This priest, seeing how wet he was, gave him some other clothes, and told him to put them on; but no sooner had he done so than he crouched down like a dog, and found that he had been changed into a tiger, and that the priest had vanished.

It now occurred to him to seize this opportunity of revenging himself upon his enemy; and away he went to his old ambush, where he found his own body lying stiff and stark.

Fearing lest it should become food for birds of prey, he guarded it carefully, until at length one day Zhuang passed by. Out rushed the tiger and sprang upon Zhuang, bidding his head off, and swallowing it upon the spot, at which Qiao Tong, the archer, turned round and shot the animal through the heart.

Just at that moment Xiang came to as though from a dream, but it was some time before he could crawl home, where he arrived to the great delight of his family, who didn't know what had become of him.

Xiang said not a word, lying quietly on the bed until some of his people came in to congratulate him on the death of his great enemy Zhuang.

Xiang then cried out, "I was that tiger," and proceeded to relate the whole story, which thus got about until it reached the ears of Zhuang's son, who immediately set to work to bring his father's murderer to justice. The magistrate, however, did not consider this wild story as sufficient evidence against him, and thereupon dismissed the case.

TALE 81
The Tipsy Turtle

A man named Feng in Lintiao one day got a turtle from a friend of his. The turtle had a white spot on its forehead and he was so struck with something in its appearance that he let it go.

One day when he was going back home from his son-in-law's, he reached the river where he let go the turtle. It was getting dark and he saw a drunken man come rolling along, attended by two or three servants.

Feng talked to him and the man replied, "I am the late magistrate of Nantu."

The drunken man got up from the ground, and led Feng along to a very nice house, quite like the establishment of a person of position.

Feng inquired what might be his name.

"I am the Eighth Prince of the Tiao river. I have just been out to take wine with a friend, and somehow I got tipsy."

A banquet followed, and the two began to dine and wine like old friends.

Before they were aware of the time they had spent eating,

the sound of a distant bell broke upon their ears and the Prince got up and said, "We cannot remain together any longer; but I will give you something by which I may in part requite your kindness to me. It must not be kept for any great length of time when you have attained your wishes, then I will receive it back again."

He spat out of his mouth a tiny man, no more than an inch high, and scratching Feng's arm with his nails until Feng felt as if the skin was gone, he quickly laid the little man upon the spot.

When he let go, the little man had already sunk into the skin, and nothing was to be seen but a cicatrix well healed over.

When all done, Feng found the Prince and the house had all disappeared together, leaving behind a great turtle which waddled down into the water, and disappeared likewise.

However, from this moment his sight became so intensely keen that he could see almost everything he could not see before - precious stones lying in the bowels of the earth.

And from below his own bedroom he dug up many hundred ounces of pure silver, upon which he lived very comfortably; and once when a house was for sale, he perceived that in it lay concealed a vast quantity of gold, so he immediately bought it, and so became immensely rich in all kinds of valuables.

The third princess in Prince Su's family was very beautiful; and Feng, who had long heard of her fame. Delighted with this picture, he put the mirror very carefully away; but in about a year his wife had let the story leak out, and the Prince, hearing of it, threw Feng into prison, and took possession of the mirror.

Feng was to be beheaded. However, he bribed one of the Prince's ladies to tell His Highness that if he would pardon him all the treasures of the earth might easily become his; whereas, on the other hand, his death could not possibly be of any advantage to the Prince.

The Prince now thought of confiscating all his goods and banishing him; but the third princess observed, that as he had already seen her, were he to die ten times over it would not give her back her lost face, and that she had much better marry him.

The Prince would not hear of this, whereupon his daughter shut herself up and refused all nourishment, at which the ladies of the palace were dreadfully alarmed, and reported it at once to the Prince.

Feng was accordingly set free.

TALE 82

A 'Male Concubine'

A man was trying to buy a concubine in Yangzhou. He visited several families and found no girls to his liking. One day, he found an old lady trying to sell her teenage daughter. She was pretty and good at many arts. The man was satisfied with her and paid a high price for her. At night, under the quilt, the man found the girl's skin creamy smooth. He touched her lower parts and was astonished to find that his new concubine was actually a boy. A swindler had bought a pretty-looking boy and disguised him as a girl. When morning came, the man sent people out to look for the lady who had sold him the boy, but she was nowhere to be found. The man was very frustrated and did not know how to handle this "male concubine." He told this story to a friend from Zhejiang who had just passed the imperial exams and was about to become an official. This friend took one look at the boy and bought him for the same price as was paid to the lady.

TALE 83

Wang's Three Previous Lives

Wang Keshou, a native of Huangmei County, Hubei, could remember his three previous lives. During his first life, he was a scholar, studying in a temple. The monk had a female horse which delivered a mule. The scholar liked the mule so much that he ran away with it. Later the scholar died. The King of Hell was very angry when he found that the scholar was greedy and violent and did a lot of evil things. He punished the scholar by making him a mule and giving him to the monk. After the mule was born, the monk loved it very much. The mule wanted to commit suicide, but could not find the right chance. When it grew up, the mule intended to jump into the valley and kill itself. On second thought, however, it was afraid that it did not live up to the monk's kindness and therefore would be punished even more seriously in Hell. So it lived out its life. Several years later, when the term of the punishment ended, the mule died. During his third life, Mr. Wang was born into a farmer's family. As soon as he was born, he could talk. His parents killed him believing that he was too strange to be human. Then he was born into Scholar Wang's family.

Scholar Wang, close to fifty years old at the time, was very happy when a son was born. The boy understood very well that he was killed in his previous life because he started talking too early. Therefore he dared not open his mouth even when he was three or four years old. People thought he was mute. One day, when his father was writing an article, a friend came, so his father put down his pen to greet his guest. The boy went to his father's study, found the unfinished article and had an urge to help complete it for his father. After his father saw the guest off and returned to his study, he asked, "Who has been in here?" His family members all told him that no one had been in. His father could not understand. The next day, he deliberately wrote a title of an article and left it on the desk. After a short while he sneaked back to his study and discovered his son had already written several lines. The boy suddenly saw his father and could not help speaking out while kneeling down to beg his father not to punish him. His father was pleased and held his hand, "You are my only son. Your ability to write compositions is a fortune of the Wang clan. Why did you keep it a secret?" After that, his father helped him to improve his writing. He became an official at an very early age and later was promoted to chief inspector of Datong, Shanxi.

TALE 84

The Baby Buffalo

A farmer in Hubei rested by the roadside after he had been to the market. A fortune-teller came to chat with him. The fortune-teller looked at his face and said, "You do not look well. Within three days, you will lose money and be punished." The farmer reasoned, "I have paid all the taxes to the government. I never quarrel with others. Why should I be punished?" The fortune-teller said, "I do not know either, but your face foretells this. You have to be careful." The farmer did not believe him and continued on his way. The next day the farmer was tending his baby buffalo in the field when a government messenger's horse passed by. The baby buffalo saw the horse and believed it was a tiger. It charged at the horse with its horns. The horse died instantly. The horse keeper took the farmer to the government. The government officials had him beaten and ordered him to compensate for the loss of the horse. Whenever buffalos see tigers, they charge after them. Therefore the buffalo sellers protected themselves with buffalos when they stayed outside for the night. When they see horses passing by in the distance, they drive buffalos away in a hurry, afraid that the buffalos will mistake the horses for tigers and attack them.

TALE   85

Saving His Mother with His Own Flesh

Le Zhong, a native of Xi'an, was born after his father's early death. His mother believed in Buddhism and did not eat any meat or drink any alcohol. When Le Zhong grew up, he was fond of drinking and did not like her mother's practices. So he often advised his mother to eat fatty meat and drink liquor. Each time, his mother rebuked him. When his mother was seriously ill, she wanted to eat meat, believing it would improve her health. Unable to find any meat at the market, Le Zhong cut out a chunk of his own flesh. Having eaten the flesh, his mother's health improved. But when she learned where the meat had come from, she regretted her action and refused to eat anything. Soon she starved to death.

Le Zhong was extremely sad. He used a sharp knife to cut his right leg so deep that bone was exposed. Family members saved him by wrapping the wound with a medicated bandage. His Leg soon healed.

Le Zhong married at the age of twenty. On the third day of his marriage, he complained, "What husbands and wives do together is the dirtiest thing in the world. I cannot find any happiness in it!" So he drove away his wife. His father-in-law, Gu Wenyuan, demanded Le Zhong's relatives speak to the boy. But no matter what they said, he refused to take back his wife. Gu Wenyuan was forced to arrange another marriage for his daughter three months later. Le Zhong lived by himself for another twenty years, during which time he became even more unrestrained, drinking with servants and artists alike. He was never tight-fisted when his neighbors or relatives asked for his assistance. A neighbor once commented that he had no iron pot to give his daughter as a wedding gift. Le Zhong took the one from his stove and gave it to the man. He had to borrow a pot from his neighbor each time he wanted to cook a meal. Several scoundrels learned of his generosity and decided to take advantage of him. One of them wept before Le Zhong, saying that he had to sell his son for paying urgent taxes. Actually the scoundrel was a gambler. Le Zhong gave the man all of his money. When the tax man came to collect from Le Zhong, he was forced to sell all of his property to pay the taxes. He became poorer and poorer as the days passed.

Le Zhong's family had been rich and prosperous. His relatives were always seeking his favor. He never refused to help them when they were in need. But as Le Zhong's fortunes began to wane, his relatives wanted nothing to do with him. Still, he did not think ill of the relatives. On the anniversary of his mother's death, he was ill and unable to attend a memorial ceremony. He asked his cousins for help, but they each offered some excuse. In the end, Le Zhong could only pay his respects to his mother by pouring wine on the ground at his home and weeping before his mother's memorial tablet. His grief was so strong that he passed out. A gentle touch awoke him to find his mother standing over him. Surprised, he asked, "What are you doing here?" His mother said, "Since no one came to my grave, I came to see what was wrong." "Where did you come from?" he asked her. His mother said she had been staying at the South Sea. Again she touched him, and his body turned cold. When he looked up again, he was alone. But his health was fully restored.

Now able to be up and about, he decided to travel to the South Sea to pray there for his mother. Several villagers were organizing a pilgrimage society. Le Zhong sold some of his land to pay for an application to join the society. However, the people in the society did not like his drinking and the fact that he ate meat. They refused has application, saying he was unclean. So Le Zhong followed behind them on their pilgrimage. Along the way, he continued to eat beef, onions, and garlic. He also drank alcohol. The others found him distasteful and sneaked off without him one evening as he lay drunk beside the road. Le Zhong had to go on alone. When he reached Fujian, a friend invited him to dinner. A famous showgirl, Qionghua, was also present. Le Zhong mentioned his trip to the South Sea and Qionghua expressed her eagerness to join him. Le Zhong was pleased. They were soon on their way. Although they ate and slept together, they never had sexual relations.

When they reached the South Sea, other people criticized him for bringing a showgirl along. They look down upon him and were unwilling to pray at the same time as he. Le Zhong and Qionghua understood their feelings and let them hold their worship ceremonies first. The Buddha did not reveal himself to the members of the pilgrimage society during their solemn religious service. But when Le Zhong and Qionghua knelt down to pray, lotus flowers appeared on the sea. Qionghua saw the Goddess of Mercy and Le Zhong saw his mother floating above the flowers. He immediately ran to his mother. The others saw tens of thousands of lotus flowers became colorful clouds hovering over the sea like a silk cloth. After a while, the clouds and waves calmed and everything disappeared, leaving Le Zhong on the shore. He did not know how he had reached the shore or why his clothes and shoes were not wet. Looking at the sea, he cried so loudly that he shook the islands. Qionghua pleaded with him to leave the shore. They hired a boat and headed north.

On their return trip, a rich family hired Qionghua to serve in their house while Le Zhong rested alone in a hotel. A young boy, no more than eight or nine years old, was begging in the hotel, although he did not look like a beggar. Le Zhong spoke with the boy and found he had been driven out of his home by his step-mother. He took pity on the boy, who was reluctant to leave the hotel and asked for Le Zhong's help. Le Zhong agreed to take the boy home with him. Le Zhong asked his family name and the boy said, "My family name is Yong and my given name is Axin. My mother's family name is Gu. My mother said that she gave birth to me only six months after she married her second husband. She said I should have been named after my real father, who was named Le." Le Zhong was very surprised to hear the boy's story. But he doubted this was his son, since he had only slept with his wife on their wedding night. He asked if the boy know where his father was from. Although he said he had no idea, his mother had given him a letter before she died and told him not to lose it. Le Zhong immediately asked to read the letter and found it was the letter of divorce he had written to his wife's family years ago. He was amazed and told the boy, "You are my son." Happy as he was, his life was becoming more and more difficult. Two years later, he was forced to sell what was left of his land and was unable to keep a young housekeeper in his employ.

One day, when the father and son were cooking, a beautiful

woman suddenly walked into the room. She was Qionghua. Le Zhong asked her, "Where did you come from?" Qionghua replied with a smile, "I have pretended to be your wife on our travels, how can you ask such a question? I did not follow you immediately since the madam was watching after me. But now she is dead. If I do not marry, I have no one to lean on. If I get married, I cannot remain chaste. But I can realize both purposes if I stay with you, since you are celibate. So I have come from a long way to join your family." She put down her luggage and cooked for the boy. Le Zhong was very cheerful. At night, the father and the son still slept in the same room. The boy regarded Qionghua as his mother and Qionghua also looked after him very well. Relatives came with food and drinks to congratulate them. Le Zhong and Qionghua accepted it with pleasure. Whenever there were guests around, Qionghua would prepare nice food and drinks. Le Zhong did not bother to ask where she found the money to buy such things. Qionghua also used her gold, silver and jewelry to buy back Le Zhong's previous properties. She also bought a lot of servants, cows and horses. The family became better off with each passing day, Le Zhong often said to Qionghua, "When I am drunk, please keep away from me and do not let me see you." Qionghua agreed with a smile. One day when Le Zhong was drunk, he called Qionghua. Qionghua came to him wearing a beautiful gown. After he looked at her for a long time, he became very excited and acclaimed, waving his hands, "Now I understand." He became very sober and found his world was in fact bright and cheerful. He realized that all his houses were beautiful and expensive buildings. From that day forward he did not go out to drink. Instead he stayed home with Qionghua. He drank while she ate vegetables and drank tea to accompany him.

One day, Le Zhong was slightly drunk and asked Qionghua

to massage his legs. Qionghua saw scars on his legs, which looked like two lotus buds protruding slightly from his skin. Le Zhong smiled and said, "When the buds are in blossom, it will be time we end our twenty years of life disguised as husband and wife." Qionghua believed what he said.

After Le Zhong's son, Axin, married, Qionghua handed the housework over to her daughter-in-law. She and Le Zhong lived in another courtyard. The son and daughter-in-law visited them once every three days, reporting only the difficult things they found hard to handle themselves. They hired two maids to serve the parents, one serving wine and the other serving tea. One day, Qionghua visited the son. The daughter-in-law spoke with her for quite a long time. Then they went together to see Le Zhong. They found him sitting in bed, barefooted. When he heard them approach, he opened his eyes slightly and said with a smile, "It's good that you've come." With that, he closed his eyes. Qionghua was startled, "Is there anything wrong?" She found that the lotus flowers on ins legs were in full blossom. She tried to feel his breath but he had stopped breathing. Qionghua placed her hands over the lotus petals and prayed, "It's not very easy for me to come from a long way to stay with you. I've been teaching your son and daughter-in-law. Why don't you wait for me for another two or three years?" After a lone while, Le Zhong suddenly opened his eyes and smiled, saying, "You have your work to do. Why do you have to drag me along? Well, for your sake, I shall remain here with you." Qionghua lifted her hands and the lotus flowers on Le Zhong's legs had become buds again. He again became his usual self, laughing and talking merrily.

Three years passed. Qionghua was almost forty years old, but she looked as if she were still in her twenties. She said to Le Zhong one day, "After ordinary people die, their bodies are handled by others. It doesn't look good and is not clean either." She ordered some carpenters to make a pair of coffins. Axin asked what she was doing and Qionghua replied, "You would not understand." When the coffins were ready, Qionghua took a bath and dressed herself. She said to their son daughter-in-law, "I am dying." Axin cried, "Mother, because you've been looking after the family so well we do not suffer from cold or hunger. You have not had a chance to enjoy life yourself. Why do you want to leave us?" Qionghua answered, "A son should enjoy the good life that his father has earned for him. In your case, the servants, cows and horses have been paid back to your father by those who cheated him. I have not done much. I was previously a fairy whose job was to scatter flowers. I came down to the earth and have been living here for over thirty years. Now my term on the earth has expired." She lay down in the coffin. Axin called to her, but her eyes were already closed. Crying, Axin went to report this to his father, only to find his father also dead. Axin was gripped by deep grief and cried sorrowfully. He put his father's body into the coffin and placed the pair of coffins in the hall without closing the covers. He hoped that they would come to life again. At this time, from Le Zhong's leg shot up a beam of light illuminating the whole room. The fragrance curling up from Qionghua's coffin was so intoxicating that even the neighbors smelled it. After the coffin covers were put in place, the fragrance and light disappeared.

After the funeral, the cousins in the Le clan were jealous of his wealth and wanted to drive away Axin. They sued Axin the county court. The court decided to award half of Axin's properties to his shiftless cousins. Axin appealed to the prefectural court. The case was before the court for a long time, without any resolution.

Years ago, Gu Wenyuan arranged for his daughter to remarry a man in the Yong clan. A year later, the Yong clan moved to Fujian and Gu lost contact with his daughter. When Gu Wenyuan was old, he missed his daughter all the more, so he went to Fujian to visit her and her husband. By the time he arrived in Fujian, his daughter was already dead and his grandson had been driven away. Gu Wenyuan sued the Yongs. The Yongs, frightened, tried to settle the case by paying him some money, which he refused. He insisted on having his grandson back. Although he had looked for his grandson everywhere, he could not find him. When Gu Wenyuan was on his way home one day, he saw a colorful carriage passing by. He made way for it by standing along the roadside. A beauty in the carriage spoke to him, "Aren't you Old Gu?" Gu Wenyuan said yes. The beauty told him, "Your grandson is my son who is living in the Le family now. You don't have to sue the Yongs. Your grandson is in difficulty and you should go and help him out immediately." Gu Wenyuan wanted to find out the details, but the carriage went away. Gu accepted the money from the Yongs and rushed to Xi'an. Le's court case was being tried when he reached there. He explained to the court his daughter's divorce date and remarriage date as well as the birthday of his grandson, making everything very clear. All the cousins of Axin were beaten and driven from the court. The case was closed.

At home, Gu Wenyuan mentioned the date on which he met the beauty and realized that it was the very day Qionghua had died. Axin moved all his grand-father's belongings to his village and offered the old man a house, a concubine and maids. Old Gu even had a son when he was over sixty. Axin took good care of his baby brother.

TALE 86

The Girl Called Fragrant Jade

At the Xiaqinggong Temple at the foot of the Laoshan Mountain in Shandong, evergreen trees grew sturdily. And peonies stood over three meters high. Huang Sheng, a native of Jiaoxian, Shandong, came to the temple to study. One day he stood in front of a window and saw a lady in a white dress moving about among the flowers. Huang Sheng wondered how there could be a woman in a Taoist temple. He rushed outside and found the lady had disappeared. In the following days Huang Sheng spotted her several times. One day, he hid himself in the woods waiting for her arrival. Soon the lady arrived in the company of a woman dressed in red. From his vantage point, he admired their exceptional beauty. As the pair approached, the woman in red stopped and said, "There is a stranger here." Huang Sheng jumped out abruptly. The two ladies ran away in a panic with their skirts and sleeves waving and scattering fragrance. Huang Sheng chased them to a short wall where they went totally out of sight. Huang Sheng loved them more and wrote a poem under a tree to express his love for them, Love can be miserable; alone I stand by the window. Fearing girls marry the noble; looking for my love, where should I go?

In his study, Huang Sheng kept thinking of the girls. One day the lady in the white dress came without notice. Huang Sheng met her warmly. The lady smiled, saying, "At first, you were so fierce that you looked like a bandit and frightened me. I did not know that you are also a sentimental poet. That's why I wanted to meet you." Huang Sheng asked about her life. She told him, "My first name is Xiangyu (meaning Fragrant Jade). Previously I had lived in a brothel. A monk in the Xiaqinggong Temple has shut me up here in the mountain. This is not at all what I want." Huang Sheng asked, "What's the name of the monk? I want to take revenge for you." Xiangyu told him it was unnecessary, saying, "He dared not to force me to go to bed with him. And it gives me a chance to meet with a passionate poet like you. This is not too bad." Huang Sheng asked who the girl in the red dress was. The lady said, "She is called Jiangxue, a sworn sister of mine." The two had intimate actions together. When they woke, it was already daylight. Xiangyu got up immediately, saying, "We enjoyed loving each other and forgot that it was already bright with daylight." She put on her clothes as she said, "I've written a poem in response to yours. Don't laugh at me. Our time together flies by; before we know it, it is already daylight. I wish we were swallows; together we would fly." Huang Sheng held her wrist and said, "You are not only beautiful, but also bright. I love you very much. If you leave me even for one day, it will be as if we have been apart forever. Please do not wait until evening, but come whenever you have a chance." Xiangyu agreed. After that, they were together day and night.

Huang Sheng asked Xiangyu to invite Jiangxue to join them, but Jiangxue did not accept the invitation. Huang Sheng regretted it and Xiangyu said, "Jiangxue is a very lonely person. She is different from me. It takes time to convince her so you don't have to do it in a hurry." One evening, Xiangyu came and she looked terrible. She said to Huang Sheng, "You can't have me any more. We now have to be apart forever." Huang Sheng asked where she would go. Xiangyu wiped her tears with her sleeve, saying, "This is fate and I can't explain it to you. Your poem now has become an unfortunate prediction." When Huang Sheng pressed for an explanation, she simply cried violently, without uttering a word. That night, she remained awake and left in the early morning. Huang Sheng was mystified by the development.

The next day a man named Lan from Jimo County toured the Xiaqinggong Temple and was struck by a white peony plant he saw. He dug up the plant to take it home. Now it dawned on Huang Sheng that Xiangyu was a peony fairy. A few days later, it was said that the white peony was replanted at Lan's home, but quickly withered with each passing day. Huang Sheng wrote fifty poems under the title Crying for the Peony. Everyday he mourned and cried at the pit left by Xiangyu .

Huang Sheng was going to return home after mourning one day when he saw the lady in red, as Jiangxue also was sobbing at the pit where the white peony used to stand. Huang went up to her and she did not flee. He pulled at Jiangxue's sleeve and cried together with her. Later Huang Sheng invited her to his room and Jiangxue agreed to go along. She sighed, "We have been sisters since childhood. Now we have to be apart from each other. When I see you so sad I feel more grieved. When she learns that we are crying for her, she will be so moved by our sincerity that she will come to life again. But until that happens, she is dead to us." Huang Sheng said, "It's my bad luck that affected her. Neither have I had the good fortune to love both of you. In the past, I asked

Xiangyu several times to convey my wishes to you. Why didn't you come?" Jiangxue replied, "I thought nine out of ten young scholars were frivolous and did not take love seriously. I did not expect you to value love so deeply. I can love you passionately, but not physically. If we make love every day and night, I cannot manage." She wanted to leave after saying this, but Huang Sheng said, "Xiangyu has left me forever and I feel uneasy all day long. I hope you can stay a bit longer to comfort me. Why do you want to leave now?" Jiangxue stayed for one night and did not come back for several days.

The cold rain drops beat against the windows, making Huang Sheng miss Xiangyu all the more. He tossed and turned in bed, unable to fall asleep. His tears drenched his pillow. He put on his clothes and lit the candle to write another poem, "Rain at dusk in a miserable mountain temple; sitting by a window, I feel miserable. Missing my lover deeply; I cry during the night all alone." While reading aloud the poem to himself, he heard someone speaking outside the window, "Since somebody has written a poem, someone must respond to it with another poem." It was Jiangxue's voice. He immediately opened the door to let her in. After reading Huang Sheng's poem, Jiangxue wrote hers, "Where is your loved one except the alone candle by the window? Though there is only one man, there is a pair in the form of shadows." Huang Sheng cried after reading the poem and blamed Jiangxue for not coming more often. Jiangxue explained, "I can't be as enthusiastic as Xiangyu. All I can do is to bring you a little consolation." Huang Sheng wanted to make love with her but Jiangxue said, "Happiness does not necessarily come from sex."

After that, whenever Huang Sheng felt lonely, Jiangxue would come. They drank and read poems together. Huang Sheng left it for her to decide whether she should stay for the night.

He said to Jiangxue, "Xiangyu was my beloved wife and you are my good friend." He often asked Jiangxue, "Which flower in the courtyard are you? Please tell me so that I can take it and plant it at my home. This way what has happened to Xiangyu will not happen to you." Jiangxue said, "It's difficult for me to leave my hometown and so there is no need to tell you which plant it is. Even your beloved wife was unable to accompany you, how can I, your friend, do it?" Huang Sheng would not listen, so he dragged her to the garden, and pointing at a peony plant, asked, "Is this you?" Jiangxue did not say anything, but smiled with her hands covering her mouth.

Soon November arrived. Huang Sheng went back home to offer sacrifices to his ancestors. In February, he saw Jiangxue in a dream. She said to him in a hurried voice, "I'm running into something that will be disastrous. You'd better come back immediately so that we can still see each other. Otherwise, it will be too late." Huang Sheng felt the dream was very strange. Nevertheless, he ordered his servants to prepare a horse and he rode to Laoshan Mountain right away. The monks in the temple wanted to build more houses. An evergreen tree was in the way and the builders wanted to cut it down. Huang Sheng immediately stopped them.

At night, Jiangxue came to express her thanks to Huang Sheng. He smiled, "You did not tell me the truth about yourself earlier. You should have had this bad luck. Now I know who you are, if you don't come, I'll burn grass near you." Jiangxue said, "I knew you would nag me so I dared not tell you before." The two sat down for a while. Huang Sheng said, "Together with my good friend, I miss my beautiful wife more. I haven't mourned for Xiangyu for a long time. Will you go and mourn her together with me?" The two then went together and wept at the pit. After more than an hour, Jiangxue stopped and also asked Huang Sheng to stop crying.

Several nights later when Huang Sheng was sitting alone, Jiangxue came in and said, "I have good news for you. The flower spirit has been moved by you so he will let Xiangyu come alive in Xiaqinggong Temple again." Huang Sheng asked when and Jiangxue answered, "I don't have any idea. I guess it will not be long." In the morning, before Jiangxue got out of bed and left, Huang Sheng told her, "I came back from home for you. Please don't leave me alone." Jiangxue agreed with a smile, but she still did not come for two nights. Huang Sheng went out and embraced the evergreen tree, shaking, touching, crying, but it had no response. Huang Sheng returned to his room and prepared some dry grass, intending to light it by the tree. Jiangxue entered abruptly and threw away the dry grass, saying, "Don't make a prank. If you burn me, I shall stop having anything to do with you." Huang Sheng embraced her warmly.

The two were about to sit down, when Xiangyu walked in. Tears came rolling down from Huang Sheng's eyes. He held one hand and Jiangxue held the other. The three sobbed together. Huang Sheng felt that holding Xiangyu's hand was like holding air and so asked her why. Xiangyu told him, "Previously I was a flower fairy, so my hand was firm, and now I am a flower ghost and I am empty. Now that we can get together, just regard it as a dream and don't take it for real." Jiangxue said, "It's so good that you have come. Your husband has been nagging me for it all the time." With that she left. Xiangyu looked and smiled the same as before, but when the two embraced together, she seemed like a shadow. Huang Sheng was unhappy. Xiangyu was also regretful. She said to Huang Sheng, "Please mix some ampelopsin with sulphur in water and water me with one cup a day. On this day next year, your love will be rewarded." Then, she also left.

The next day, Huang Sheng went to the place where the white peony used to grow. He saw a peony shoot had come out. He tended it everyday, banking it with earth and also protecting it with a fence. Xiangyu was grateful to Huang Sheng. He wanted to move the baby peony to his house but Xiangyu did not agree, saying, "I am so weak that I cannot be damaged any more. Everything grows in its own place. I was not intended to grow at your place in this time. Life will be shortened if fate is not followed. As long as you love me, the day when we can be together will arrive." Huang Sheng complained that Jiangxue did not come visiting him. Xiangyu said, "If you insist on her coming, I have an idea." She and Huang Sheng took a lantern to the evergreen tree. She found a piece of grass, measured it with her palm and then measured the tree with the grass. When she measured from the bottom up to a certain position, she pointed at it and asked Huang Sheng to tickle the place with two fingers. Jiangxue came from the back of the tree immediately. She protested to Xiangyu with a smile, "So you have come with him to do evil things!" The two pulled Jiangxue to their room. Xiangyu said, "Don't be angry. Please look after him for a while. We will not trouble you again one year from now." As she promised, Jiangxue came more often after this. Huang Sheng observed the baby peony grow day by day. At the end of spring, its height was almost one meter. When Huang Sheng was away at home, he paid the monks to water the peony everyday. The next April, when Huang Sheng came back to the Xiaqinggong Temple, he saw a flower with a bud about to bloom. Reluctant to leave the peony, he watched the bud turn into a blossom. The flower was huge and a small beauty sat in the middle of the flower. The beauty climbed doom. It was Xiangyu, who said to Huang Sheng, "I was beaten by rain and wind and you came so late." They went inside the house. Jiangxue arrived as well and said with a smile, "I acted everyday as a wife on your behalf. And I am happy to return to my position of a friend." The three chatted together while drinking. At midnight, Jiangxue left. The couple slept together as before.

After Huang Sheng's wife died, he came to the mountain to stay. The stem of the peony was as thick as a human arm. Huang Sheng often said, "After I die, my spirit will remain here on your left side." Both Xiangyu and Jiangxue said to him, "Please keep your word."

A dozen years later, Huang Sheng became suddenly ill. His son came to see him, gripped by sadness. Huang Sheng smiled, "I shall have a new life. Don't be sad." He said to the monk. "Under the peony, there will be a red baby peony with five leaves. That will be me." He said nothing more. His son carried him home on a carriage. Soon he died. The next year a baby peony grew beside the white peony. It was just as Huang Sheng had described it. The Taoist monk found it so strange that he watered it with great care. Three years later, it grew to one meter and was very strong. But it bore no flowers. After the old monk passed away, his students did not value the plant so they cut it doom. The white peony withered. Soon the evergreen tree died too.

TALE   87

The Magic Path

Guo was a young man born and brought up in Guang-dong. One day, when he was returning home after a visit to a friend of his, he lost his way in a hill.

He wandered about in a thick jungle for an hour, and suddenly heard the sound of laughing and talking on the top of the hill. Hurrying up in the direction of the sound, he saw a dozen persons dining and wining there.

Being invited, Guo sat down with the company, and found most of them belonged to the literati.

These people were all full of fun, and could imitate exactly the note of any kind of birds. Guo began on the sly to twitter like a swallow, to the great astonishment of the others, and then changed his note to that of a cuckoo, sitting there laughing and saying nothing.

After a while he imitated a parrot, and cried, "Mr. Guo is very drunk. You'd better see him home," and all burst out laughing.

They screwed up their mouths and tried to whistle like Guo, but none of them could do so. Soon one of them observed, "What a pity Madam Qing isn't with us, we must rendezvous here again at mid-autumn, and you, Mr. Guo, must be sure and come."

Guo said he would, whereupon another of his hosts got up and remarked that, as he had given them such an amusing entertainment, they would try to show him a few acrobatic feats.

They all arose, and one of them planting his feet firmly, a second jumped up on to his shoulders, a third on to the second's shoulders, and a fourth on to his, until it was too high for the rest to jump up, and accordingly they began to climb as though it had been a ladder.

When they were all up, and the topmost head seemed to touch the clouds, the whole column bent gradually down until it lay along the ground transformed into a path. Guo remained for some time in a state of considerable alarm, and then, setting out along this path, ultimately reached his own home.

Some days afterwards he revisited the spot, and saw the remains of a feast lying about on the ground, with dense bushes on all sides, but no sign of a path. At mid-autumn he thought of keeping his engagement; however, his friends persuaded him not to go.

TALE 88

A Faithless Widow

In Jiangxi there was man named Niu, who traded in piece goods. They had two children, a boy and a girl. Life was happy, but he died at thirty-three years of age when his son Chung was only twelve and his daughter eight or nine.

Niu's wife sold off all the property, pocketed the proceeds and married another man, leaving her two children almost in a state of destitution with their aunt, Niu's sister-in-law, an old lady of sixty, who had lived with them previously, and had now nowhere to seek a shelter.

A few years later this aunt died, and the family fortunes began to sink even lower than before. Chung, now grown-up man, was determined to carry on his father's trade, but he had no capital to start with.

He borrowed ten ounces of silver from his sister, who had married a rich trader named Mao, and immediately started for Nanjing.

On the road he fell in with some bandits, who robbed him of all he had, and consequently he was unable to return. One day when he was at a pawnshop he noticed that the master of the shop was wonderfully like his late father, and on going out and making inquiries he found that this pawnbroker bore precisely the same names.

In great astonishment, he forthwith proceeded to frequent the place with no other object than to watch this man, who, on the other hand, took no notice of Chung.

Three days later, having satisfied himself that he really saw his own father, and yet not daring to disclose his own identity, he made application through one of the assistants, on the score of being himself a Jiangxi man, to be employed in the shop.

When the master noticed Chung's name and place of residence he started, he asked him whence he came.

With tears in his eyes Chung addressed him by his father's name, and then the pawnbroker became lost in a deep reverie.

Chung said, "My father went away on business six years ago, and never came back; my mother married again..."

The pawnbroker was much moved, and cried out, "I am your father!"

Seizing his son's hand, he him within to see his step-mother.

This lady was about twenty-two, and they no children of their own. The woman was delighted with Chung, and prepared a banquet for him in the inner apartments.

Niu himself was somewhat melancholy, and wished to return to his old home; but his wife, fearing that there would be no one to manage the business, persuaded him to remain.

Niu taught his son all about the trade, and in three months as able to leave it all to him and prepared for his journey.

At this point of time, Chung told his step mother that his father was really dead, but the woman said she knew him only as a trader to the place, and that six years previously he had married her, which proved conclusively that he couldn't be dead.

Next day, his father came to his room together with a woman whose hair was all dishevelled. She was his own mother; and Niu took her by the ear and began to revile her, saying, "Why did you desert my children?"

All of a sudden, Chung's mother disappeared in a minute, and Niu himself became a black vapor and also vanished from their sight.

The step-mother and Chung buried Niu's clothes, and after that Chung continued his father's business, and soon amassed great wealth. On returning to his native place he found that his mother had actually died on the very day of the above occurrence, and that his father had been seen by the whole family.

TALE 89

Bee Princess Lily

Tou Shan, also known as Xiaohui, was a native of Qiaozhou. One day he dreamed of a man in serge clothes who invited him to follow him to a place with many white houses shaded by lemon-trees. They threaded their way past countless doors, not at all similar to those usually used. A great many official-looking men and women there called out to the man in serge, "Has Mr. Tou come?"

A mandarin took Tou into a palace and said, "Our Prince has long heard of you as a man of good family and excellent principles, and is very anxious to make your acquaintance."

Just then out came two girls with banners, who guided Tou to a throne, upon which sat the Prince. His Highness immediately descended to meet him, and made him take the seat of honor.

When the wine had gone round several times there arose from a distance the sound of pipes and singing, unaccompanied, however, by the usual drum, and very much subdued in volume.

The Prince cried out, "We are about to set a verse for any

of you gentlemen to cap; here you are,- Genius seeks the Cassia Court."

Tou added, "Refinement loves the Lily flower."

The Prince exclaimed, "How strange! Lily is my daughter's name; and, after such a coincidence, she must come in for you to see her."

In a few moments the tinkling of her ornaments and a delicious fragrance of musk announced the arrival of the Princess, who was between sixteen and seventeen, and endowed with surpassing beauty.

Tou remained in a state of stupefaction, and the Prince, perceiving what had distracted his guest's attention, remarked that he was anxious to find a consort for his daughter.

Tou started to recover himself at once, rose from the table and apologized to the Prince for his rudeness.

The sun had already set, and there he sat in the gloom thinking of what had happened. In the evenings, all he could do was to pour forth his repentance in sighs.

One night he dreamed to see an officer of the Court summoned him to appear before the Prince. The Princess came in, a red veil covering her head. They slept in the same room.

Next morning Tou amused himself by helping the Princess to paint her face, and then with a girdle he began to measure the size of her waists and with his fingers the length of her feet.

"Are you crazy?" cried she, laughing; to which Tou replied. "I have been deceived so often by dreams, that I am now making a careful record. If such it turns out to be, I shall still have something as a souvenir of you."

All of a sudden, a great monster got into the palace. The Prince grasped his hand and, with tears in his eyes, begged him not to desert them.

The Prince told Tou, "A report has just been received from the officer in charge of the Yellow Gate stating that, ever since the 6th of the 5th lunar moon, a huge monster, some 10,000 feet in length, had devoured 13,800 people outside palace."

The Prince begged Tou to look to his own safety without regarding the wife through whom he was involved in their misfortunes.

The Princess, however, begged Tou not to desert her. After a moment's hesitation, he said he should be only too happy to place his own poor home at their immediate disposal if they would only deign to honor him.

When all of a sudden he awoke and found that it was all a dream.

Tou still heard a buzzing in his ears which he knew was not made by any human being, and, on looking carefully about, he discovered two or three bees which had settled on his pillow.

When he told his friend all about this, his friend advised him to get a hive for them, which he did without delay; and immediately it was filled by a whole swarm of bees, which came flying from over the wall in great numbers.

TALE 90

The Donkey Revenges

Chung Qingyu in Manchuria was told a Taoist priest at the capital could tell people's fortunes, and was very anxious to see him about his future.

When he traveled a long distance there, he found around the priest stood a perfect wall of people inquiring their future fortunes, and to each the old man made a brief reply. When he saw Chung among the crowd, he was overjoyed, and, seizing him by the hand, said, "Sir, your virtuous intentions command my esteem."

"You may succeed passing this examination," said the priest, "but on returning covered with honor to your home, I fear that your mother will be no longer there."

Chung was a very filial son. When he heard these words, his tears began to flow, and he declared that he would go back without competing any further.

The priest took out a pill and told Chung that if he has it sent to his mother, it would prolong her life for seven days, and thus he would be able to see her once again after the examination was over.

Chung took the pill, and went off in very low spirits; but he soon reflected that the span of human life is a matter of destiny, and that every day he could spend at home would be one more day devoted to the service of his mother.

Accordingly, he hired a donkey, and set out on his way back. When he had gone about half-a-mile, the donkey turned round and ran home; and when he used his whip, the animal threw itself down on the ground.

The sun was now sinking behind the hills, and his servant advised his master to stay and finish his examination while he himself went back home before him.

Chung had no alternative but to assent, and the next day he hurried through with his papers, starting immediately afterwards, and not stopping at all on the way either to eat or to sleep. All night long he went on, and arrived to find his mother in a very critical state.

When he gave her the pill she so far recovered that he was able to go in and see her. Grasping his hand, she begged him not to weep, telling him that she had just dreamt she had been down to the Infernal Regions, where the King of Hell had informed her with a gracious smile that her record was fairly clean, and that in view of the filial piety of her son she was to have twelve years more of life.

Before long the news arrived that Chung had passed his examination. He bade adieu to his mother, and went off to the capital, where he bribed the eunuchs of the palace to communicate with his friend the Taoist priest. The priest was very much pleased, and came out to see him, whereupon Chung prostrated himself at his feet.

The priest predicted, "You will never rise to high rank, but you will attain the years of an octogenarian. In a former state of existence you and I were once travelling together, when you threw a stone at a dog, and accidentally killed a frog."

The priest went on to say, "Now that frog has reappeared in life as a donkey, and according to all principles of destiny you ought to suffer for what you did; but your filial piety has moved the Buddha."

Later, Chung married a young lady, who was sixteen years of age, and very beautiful. They enjoy a happy life.

TALE 91

Wolf Dream

One day a man named Ding paid a visit to Bai in Zhili as the two had not seen each other for a long time.

Ding was one of those persons who are occasionally employed by the Judge of the Infernal Regions to make arrests on earth. Ding told him all kinds of strange things, but Bai did not believe them, answering only by a smile.

One day, Bai was ready to take a nap when Ding asked him to go for a walk.

When they saw a majestic house, Ding said, "That's where your nephew works and lives."

Ding was mentioning the son of Bai's elder sister, who was a magistrate in Hunan. They walked in and found Bai's nephew was sitting in his court dressed in his official robes. Around him stood so many guards that it was impossible to get close to him.

Bai said his son lived nearby, and asked Ding if he would like to see him too.

Before long, they came to a large building guarded by a fierce wolf at the entrance. They walked in. Ding found all the house ser-

vants were standing about and others lying down to sleep. They were all wolves!

When Bai's son, Chia, saw his father accompanied by Ding, he was overjoyed, and, asking them to sit down, bade the attendants serve some refreshments.

A big wolf brought in his mouth the carcase of a dead man, and set it before them. Bai rose up in consternation, and asked his son what this meant.

"It's only a little refreshment for you, father," replied Chia.

A general stampeded among the animals. He looked sternly at Chia, and, producing a black rope, proceeded to bind him hand and foot. Chia fell down before them, and was changed into a tiger with horrid fangs...

Well, Bai found he had been dreaming, and at once set off to invite Ding to come and see him; but Ding said he must beg to be excused.

Bai pondered on what he had seen in his dream, and despatched his second son with a letter to Chia, full of warnings and good advice. The reply was that Bai's eldest son had lost all his front teeth when he had a fall from his horse when tipsy.

In the next year, Chia had been given a post in the Board of Civil Office, but the old man sighed.

A few days later, a message came to say that Chia had fallen in with bandits while on his way home, and that he and all his reti-nue had been killed. The survivors say Chia had fallen in with ban-dits, who cried out, "We have come to avenge the cruel wrongs of many hundreds of victims."

Bai arose and immediately proceeded to burn incense. Some of his friends would have persuaded him that the report was prob-ably untrue; but the old man had no doubts as to its correctness, and made haste to get ready his son's grave.

TALE 92

The Wronged Case

Chu was a native of Yangku, who, has lost his wife not long before their marriage. One day, he went off to ask an old woman to arrange another match for him.

Chu fell in with a neighbor's wife, who took his fancy very much. One day he said in joke to the matchmaker, "Get me that stylish-looking, handsome lady, and I shall be quite satisfied."

"I'll see what I can do," replied the old woman, also joking, "if you will manage to kill her present husband." Chu laughed and said he certainly would do so.

A month afterwards, the said husband was actually killed in a lonely spot when he went out working. The local magistrate summoned the neighbors for clue about the killing, and the matchmaker told the magistrate about her conversation with Chu, who was soon arrested.

The magistrate also suspected the wife of the murdered man, and accordingly, she was severely beaten and tortured and she falsely acknowledged her guilt.

Chu was then examined, and he said, "This delicate woman

could not bear the agony of your tortures; what she has stated is untrue. I killed the husband that I might secure the wife. She knew nothing at all about it."

When asked for some proof, Chu said his bloody clothes would be evidence enough, but no bloody clothes were forthcoming.

He was then beaten till he fainted; yet when he came round he still stuck to what he had said. There was now no doubt as to the truth of Chu's story; and as nothing occurred to change the magistrate's opinion, Chu was thrown into prison to await the day for his execution.

Meanwhile, as the magistrate was one day inspecting his gaol, suddenly a man appeared in the hall, who glared at him fiercely and roared out, "You are as dull-headed fool!"

The magistrate was frightened out of his wits, and tried to escape, but the man cried out to him, "Freeze! If you move an inch you are lost."

So the magistrate stood still, shaking from head to foot with fear, while the man continued, "The murderer is Kung Piao, Chu had nothing to do with it."

The man then fell down on the ground, and was to all appearance lifeless. After a while he recovered, his face having quite changed, and when he was asked about his name, he said he was Kung Piao. How he had got into the magistrate's hall he was quite unable to say.

The magistrate was lost in amazement at all this. Unfortunately for him, the reversal of his sentence cost him his appointment, and he died in poverty, unable to find his way home. As for Chu, the widow of the murdered man married him in the following year, out of gratitude for his noble behavior.

TALE 93
A Rip Van Winkle

Chia was a young man who, believe it or not, passed local imperial examination with the assistance of a mysterious Taoist friend. He was now determined to devote himself to the practice of Taoism, in the hope of obtaining the elixir of immortality.

One early morning, Chia and his friend, Lang, stole away together to a monastery in a mountain without the awareness of their families.

Chia was then escorted by Lang to a dorm, where he was provided with food, after which Lang went away. Chia took off his shoes and lay down. When he felt hungry, he tried one of the cakes on the table, which he found sweet and very satisfying.

Chia thought Lang would be sure to come back, but he hadn't. He also found that the room was fragrant with a delicious perfume, and every one of his veins and arteries could be easily counted.

Before long, a beautiful young girl came in, suffusing an exquisite fragrance around; and going up to the couch where Chia was, she bent over him and whispered, "Here I am."

Her breath was like the sweet odor of perfumes, but as Chia

did not move, she whispered again, "Are you sleeping?" The voice sounded to Chia remarkably like that of his wife. However, he reflected that these were all probably nothing more than tests of his determination, so he closed his eyes firmly for a while.

The young lady called him by his pet name, and then he opened his eyes wide to discover that she was no other than his own wife. On asking her how she had come there, she replied that Lang was afraid her husband would be lonely.

Just then they heard the old man outside in a towering rage, and Chia's wife jumped over a low wall and disappeared.

In came the old man, and Lang led Chia away over the low wall, saying, "Good-bye, but we shall meet again some day."

He then showed Chia the way to his home. Before long he was at his own door, but he noticed that the place was all tumble-down and in ruins, and not as it was when he went away. As for the people he saw, old and young alike, he did not recognize one of them.

Chia asked a man which was his house, he replied, "This is it. You probably wish to hear the extraordinary story connected with the family? I know all about it. They say that Mr. Chia ran away just after he had taken imperial examination degree, when his son was only seven or eight years old. About seven years afterwards the child's mother went into a deep sleep from which she did not awake. As long as her son was alive he changed his mother's clothes for her according to the seasons, but when he died, her grandsons fell into poverty, and had nothing but an old shanty to put the sleeping lady into. Last month she awaked, having been asleep for over a hundred years."

The eldest grandson was dead; and the second, a man of about fifty, refused to believe that such a young-looking man was really his grandfather; but in a few moments out came Chia's wife, and she recognized her husband at once.

TALE 94

Zhou Gozhang and His Ghost

Zhou Tianyi in Huanshang aged fifty had only one son, named Gozhang. This boy, thirteen, was well-favored fellow, strangely averse to study, and often playing truant from school, sometimes for the whole day, without any remonstrance on the part of his father.

One day he was found he had not come back home from school in the evening. Late that night, Gozhang returned, saying that he had been beguiled away by a Taoist priest. The priest had not done him any harm, and he found his way home himself.

From then on, he was taught at home. In the following year he passed the local imperial examination, and many of the neighbors wanted to have him as the son-in-law. Among others proposed was a nice girl, the daughter of a gentleman named Zhao, who had also passed regional imperial examination.

Gozhang's father was satisfied with the girl and her family situation. However, Gozhang wanted to continue his study and refused to marry.

One day, he was said to have been killed on his road to the

capital for imperial examination, but one day Gozhang arrived, accompanied by a retinue of horses and servants, his story being that he had formerly been kidnapped and sold to a wealthy trader. The businessman had no children and therefore adopted him, but, when he subsequently had a son born to him by his own wife, he sent Gozhang back to his old home.

Gozhang's father questioned him as to his studies, his utter dullness and want of knowledge soon made it clear that he was the real Gozhang of old, but he was already known as a man who had passed the local examination (that is, the ghost of him had not), so it was determined in the family to keep the whole affair secret.

TALE 95

The Injustice of The Heaven

Xu was a Shandong magistrate. One of his chambers was used as a store-room. To his surprise, he found creature often managed to make havoc among the stores. His servants were always scolded for this.

One day, a servant found a huge spider and hurried off to tell their master. Xu thought it so strange that he ordered the servants to feed it with cakes. Gradually, the spider would always come forth when hungry, returning as soon as it had taken enough to eat.

Years later, Xu was working in his study when suddenly the spider appeared and ran under the table. Xu gave it a cake, but he noticed it had two snakes lying on both sides.

The spider drew in its legs as if in mortal fear, and the snakes began to swell out. Xu was greatly alarmed, and would have hurried away, when a thunder hit the place, killing every person in the house except Xu.

Xu himself recovered consciousness after a little while, but only to see his wife and servants, seven persons in all, lying dead.

TALE 96

A Disembodied Friend

When the man named Chen from Shuntian Fu was a boy of sixteen, he studied at a Buddhist temple, home to a great many scholar students, including one named Chu hailing from Shandong.

Chu was diligent student who studied all day long and slept in the schoolroom. Chen became much attached to him. One day, when Chen asked Chu why he did not back home to sleep, Chu said, "I came from a poor family which can hardly afford to pay for my schooling. If I can work half the night, two of my days are equal to three of others."

Chen brought his own bed to the school, and said he would sleep there together. Chu said they would be able to do better if they put themselves under an old scholar named Lu. They succeeded to do so.

Lu was a man of considerable literary attainments, but was pinched in cash. He was delighted at getting two more pupils.

Toward the end of the first month, Chu asked for leave of absence to the astonishment of all. Dozens of days had passed by, there was no news about him at all. One day, Chen chanced to visit the Tianrun temple, and saw Chu there cutting wood.

Chen asked him why he had given up his studies; and Chu said he was so poor that he was forced to work half a month to scrape together funds enough for his next month's schooling.

"Go back with me," cried Chen. "I'll manage to pay for your schooling."

Chen agreed to go back to the school but he asked Chen to keep the whole thing a profound secret.

Chen's father, a wealthy tradesman, did not like his son would have a friend who spent his money. The man went so far as to call his son a fool, and would not let Chen resume his studies. Chu was much hurt, and would have left the school too. When Teacher Lu discovered what had taken place, he gave Chu money for him to repay Chen's father, so that he could continue his study.

Later, when Chu met Chen in street, he tried to treat him to good food at a restaurant, but Chu invariably refused.

Two years later, Chen's father died, and Chen went back to his books under the guidance of Teacher Lu, and found he was now far behind Chu. In about six months Teacher Lu's son came to beg his father to go back home, Teacher Lu had no way out but to return home with a purse his pupils had made up for him.

Teacher Lu advised Chen to take Chu as his tutor, and this he did, establishing him comfortably in the house with him.

When the imperial examination was about to commence, Chen felt convinced that he should not get through, but Chu said he should be able to give him help.

Chu introduced Chen to a gentleman named Liu, a cousin of his, for the review of lessons. Chen was put into the inner room for intensive study.

A few days afterwards Liu said to him, "A great many people

will be at the gardens today let us go and amuse ourselves awhile."

Once there, Liu brought a famous singing-girl named Li to join them. With a forced smile, Li gave them a love-song. Chen seized her hand, and said, "There's that song of the Huansha River, which you sang once before; I have read it over several times, but have quite forgotten the words." Li sang it again.

Before long, Chen found a man fell down on the ground, and Chen discovered that the one who had fallen down was really no other than himself.

When he got up, he saw Chu standing by his side, and said, "Don't be alarmed. I am nothing more than a disembodied spirit. My time for reappearing on earths is long overdue, but I could not forget your great kindness to me, and accordingly I have remained under this form in order to assist in the accomplishment of your wishes."

They then bade each other adieu. When morning came, Chen set off to call on Li, the singing-girl; but on reaching her house he found that she had been dead some days.

Towards evening Chu reappeared in high spirits, saying he had come to wish Chen a long farewell.

After the imperial examination, Chen found his name among the successful candidates whereupon he immediately started off to visit Teacher Lu to report the news.

TALE 97

A Cloth Merchant

A cloth merchant visited an old temple in Qingzhou. It was in ruins, and he came across a priest in a tumbled-down hall of Buddha. This merchant consented to do. The priest invited him to a private hall where he treated him with much courtesy.

The merchant proposed that the cloth merchant undertook the general ornamentation of the place both inside and out, but the merchant said he could not afford the expense. Because of this, the priest got very angry, and urged him so strongly that at last the merchant, in terror, promised to donate all the money he had.

When the merchant was about to leave, the priest said he should not go because he had not given the money. Moreover, he seized a knife to threat the life of the merchant, who was forced to be allowed to hang himself.

The priest then led the merchant into a dark room, and told him to make haste about it when a general happened to pass by the temple. He dismounted from his horse, and entered the temple.

The dark room was locked, and the priest refused to open it, saying the place was haunted.

The General burst open the door, and cut the merchant down at once.

The general then cut off the priest's head and set the merchant free. Later, the merchant put the temple in thorough repair, and kept it well supplied with lamps and incense ever afterwards.

TALE 98
Boat Girl Bride

Wang Gui'an was one day travelling southwards. He had moored his boat to the bank when he saw in another boat close to his a young boat girl embroidering shoes. He was just beautiful, and Wang continued gazing at her for some time, though she took not the slightest notice of him.

Minutes later, she raised her head and glanced at him, and then she continued her embroidery as before. To attract her attention, Wang threw a piece of silver toward her, but the girl picked it up and flung it on to the river bank.

A few minutes later, her

father appeared, much to the dismay of Wang. So Wang got into his own boat, and started off in pursuit of the girl's boat.

When evening came, Wang could see nothing of the boat.

Wang then did his own business and, days later, he returned on the same way, but he didn't see that girl. He then stayed put where he met the girl.

Some six months passed away, he was obliged to go home. One night he dreamed that he entered a village on the river bank, and saw a beautiful girl there.

Overjoyed at seeing her, Wang was on the point of grasping her hand, when suddenly the girl's father arrived. All of a sudden, Wang waked up, and found that it was all a dream.

In Qinjiang, the local official, named Xu, invited Wang for a visit. On his way there, Wang lost his way, and reached a village seemingly familiar to him.

It dawned to him this is the place he saw in dream. And finally he saw the boat girl there!

She jumped up on his arrival, and begged to know his name and family.

Wang said, "I should, indeed, have been married long ago."

Three days after the marriage, Wang bade adieu to his father-in-law, and started on his way northwards. They set off together towards Wang's home.

TALE 99
Two Brides

Chisheng was one of the cleverest young fellows in the area where he was born and brought up. His father and mother had foreseen his ability even when he was a baby. At eight or nine he could compose impressive poems, and by fourteen he succeeded in passing the local imperial examination.

When his father's younger sister Erniang and her husband named Cheng Zujiao had a daughter called Kueixiu. She was extremely pretty, and Chisheng fell deeply in love with the girl so that he became dangerously ill.

Chisheng's parents proposed their son's marriage with Kueixiu to her parents, but her father said No to this.

Chang living nearby had five daughters. All girls were pretty, and the youngest, called Wugo, was the most beautiful.

One day, as Wugo was on her way to worship at the family tombs, she chanced to see Chisheng. She mentioned this to her mother, and the old lady guessed what her meaning was, and arranged with a matchmaker, named Yu, to call upon Chisheng's parents. This she did precisely at the time when Chisheng was ill and was taking medicine.

When told of the proposal, Chisheng said, "There's no medicine under the Heaven that will do me any good."

Matchmaker Yu proceeded to expatiate by speaking and gesticulating on the beauty and liveliness of Wugo, but all Chisheng said was that she was not what he wanted. Turning round his face to the wall, he would listen to no more about her.

Yu was obliged to go away, and Chisheng became worse in his health. One day, all of a sudden, one of house maids came in and informed him that a young lady was at the door.

Chisheng jumped up and ran out, but he found the girl was not Kueixiu. The girl wore a light yellow robe with a fine silk jacket and an embroidered petticoat, from beneath which her two little feet peeped out. Altogether she more resembled a fairy than anything else.

It was a dream, but so accurately defined in all its details that he began to think if Wugo was really such as he had seen her, there would be no further need to try for his impracticable cousin.

Chisheng told his dream to his mother, and she was very delighted to notice this change of feeling.

When the matchmaker reached Wugo's home, the girl was ill in bed, and lay with her head propped up by pillows, looking very pretty indeed. Her mother said Wugo said she would have none but Chisheng.

When he finally saw her in person, he saw that she was truly the young lady he saw in his dream. He could hardly contain himself for joy. There he told his father and mother, who sent off a matchmaker to arrange the preliminaries; but the matchmaker came back and told them that Wugo was already betrothed. This was a terrible blow for Chisheng, who was soon as ill as ever, and offered no reply to his father and mother when they charged him with having made a mistake.

Chisheng's parents sent one to see Wugo with a letter next day, and returned to say Wugo actually vowed to married Chisheng.

Chisheng now rapidly recovered his health, and thought no more of his cousin.

One day, after the marriage, Chisheng asked Wugo why she had refused his offer, and Wugo said that she replied that was merely to pay him out for having previously refused her proposal.

"Before you had seen me, your head was full of your cousin," said Chisheng.

TALE 100

A Supernatural Wife

A Changshan man named Zhao lodged one cay visited his friend named Tai and stayed overnight there. In the morning next day, he was fatally sick. He was moved into the verandah for cooler environment. There, he saw a beautiful girl who said, "I will be your wife."

The girl promised to cure him. She rubbed his back and sides with her hand, and Changshan felt a ball of fire burning inside his body and soon began to feel much better. He asked the young lady what her name so as to remember her in his prayers.

"I am a spirit," replied the young lady. "When you lived in the Han dynasty as Chu Suilang, you were a benefactor of my family."

Zhao was ashamed of his poverty-stricken state, and afraid that his dirty room would spoil the young lady's dress, but she just walked into his apartment, where there were neither chairs nor food.

From then on, the two lived together as a family. The young lady always accompanied Zhao when he went out to dinner anywhere.

One day the couple met an unprincipled young graduate who did too much to them, she struck him on the side of the head, causing his head to fly out of the window while his body remained inside...

His head didn't return until sometime later.

TALE 101
Chinese Version of Jonah

The sky was covered with dark clouds. Suddenly, a thunder bolt hit a ship. A man named Sun Pichen was tossed about fearfully.

At this point of time, an angel in golden armor appeared in the clouds above them, holding in his hand a scroll with words reading Sun Pichen written in gold.

The angle said to Sun, "You have evidently offended the Heaven. Now get into a boat by yourself, and do not involve us in your punishment."

Without giving him time to reply, other people on the boat pushed him over the side into a small boat and set it adrift. When Sun Pichen looked back, oh, my God! the ship itself had capsized.

TALE 102

A Devoted Taoist

When the wife of Chu Yaoju, a Qingzhou man, had died, he left home for a place no one knew where it was. Some years afterwards he returned, but dressed in the Taoist garb. He stayed at home for one night and said he would leave soon.

However, his friends refused to give him his luggage, including his cassock and staff. He pretended to take a walk outside the village, and, without the awareness of others, he rushed back home and took his belongings and flied out of the house and went away swiftly.

TALE 103
Theft of Peach

The Spring Festival is the most important festival celebrated in China. In old days, on the day before, or the
Lunar New Year's Eve, all the merchants should proceed with banners and drums to the judge's yamen in a way called "bringing in
the Spring."

By then, the crowd would be immense, and the local officials
wore crimson robes and stood right and left in the hall. There was
the hum of voices and the noise of the drums.

I was present on the occasion and saw the performance in
my own eyes.

At that day there was a man leading a boy with his hair hanging down his back who walked up to the dais. The man carried a
pole on his shoulder, and appeared to be saying something which
others couldn't hear because of the noise.

One of the officials, milling from ear to ear, came down, and
in a loud voice ordered the man to give a performance.

"What shall it be?" asked the man in reply.

The official discussed on the dais with the others, and then told an attendant what the man could do best.

The man said he could invert the order of nature and produce some peaches.

Taking off his coat, he laid it on his box, at the same time observing that they had set him a hard task. As the winter frost had not broken up, he was afraid he was not able to produce peaches.

The man then proceeded to take from his box a cord some tens of feet in length, and then threw one end of it high up into the air, and the rope kept going up higher and higher until the end he had thrown up disappeared in the clouds.

He then asked his son to climb up at once. The boy seized the rope and swarmed up, like a spider running up a thread of its web. In a few moments he was out of sight in the clouds.

Then a segment of the rope and a peach came down with a run, and this affrighted the father, "someone has cut the rope! What will my boy do now?"

In another minute, his son's head came down.

The father wept bitterly and showed the audience his son's head.

"The gardener has caught him, and my boy is no more."

After that, his son's arms, legs, and body all came down, and the father, gathering them up, put them in the box and

said, "This was my only son, and I must go and bury him."

He then said to the officials, "The peach comes at the cost of my boy's life. Please be so kind as to help pay his funeral expenses."

The officials, who had been watching the scene in horror, collected a purse for him, and when he had received the money, he rapped on his box and said, "Why don't you come out and thank the gentlemen?"

When the father had finished his words, his son jumped out and bowed to the audience.

TALE 104

Adventure on a Sea Island

Kuchi Island was covered with camellias of varied colors which bloomed throughout the year. The environment was beautiful, but no one lived there, and, moreover, very few people had visited it.

One day, a young man named Chang came for hunting and adventure. The flowers were just then even finer than usual, and their perfume was diffused for a mile or so around. Many of the trees he saw were several armfuls in circumference.

Chang roamed about and gave himself up to enjoyment of the scene. While he opened a flask of wine and began to drink alone, a most beautiful young girl dressed in red stepped down from one of the camellias in front of him.

Chang was somewhat alarmed by her presence, and asked her where she came from. She told Chang she had come together with a man named Hai. When asked where Hai was, she said Hai was out for a stroll.

Chang invited her to join him in drinking and she agreed. They were just beginning to enjoy themselves when a sound of rushing wind was heard. The trees and plants bent beneath it.

"Here's Hai!" cried the young lady.

Jumping quickly up, she disappeared in a moment.

Chang was horrified to see a huge serpent swimming out of the bushes nearby, and immediately ran behind a large tree for shelter in the hope that the reptile would not see him. The serpent had sharp eyes, and moved quickly to envelope both Chang and the tree in its great folds, binding Chang's arms down to his sides so as to prevent him from moving them.

The serpent then raised its head, darted out its tongue and bit the poor man's nose, causing the blood to flow freely out, while Chang thought that his last hour had come.

Suddenly, Chang remembered he had the fox poison in his pocket, and managed to draw out the packet and managed to mix his blood with the powder for the serpent to drink.

In a few minutes, the serpent's grip was relaxed, and the huge snake struck the ground heavily with its tail and died.

Chang got up and carried the serpent off with him. He was very ill for more than a month afterwards, and even suspected the young lady of being a serpent, too, in disguise.

TALE   105

The Corpse Killer

An old man lived in a village which was located some miles from a town, where his son ran an inn to accommodate travelers.

One day, four travelers came and asked for a night's lodging. When the landlord told them all beds were occupied, the four declared it was impossible for them to go back, and urged him to take them in somehow. The landlord then said he could give them a place to sleep in if they were not too particular.

The old man's daughter-in-law had just died. Her body had not yet been buried, and her husband had gone away to buy a coffin.

The landlord took them to a room and placed a lamp on the table. At the further end of the room lay the corpse, decked out with funerals. At the foremost part of the room were sleeping couches for four people.

The four were tired, and went to bed early. All of a sudden, one of them heard a creaking of the trestles on which the dead body was laid out. He was horrified to see the dead woman was raising the coverings from her and preparing to get down.

Now she was on the floor and moving towards the sleepers. Her face was of a light yellow color, with a silk kerchief round her head. When she reached the beds, she blew on the other three travelers, whereupon the fourth, in a great fright, stealthily drew up the bed-clothes over his face, and held his breath to listen. He heard her breathe on him as she had done on the others, and then heard her go back again and get under the paper robes, which rustled distinctly as she did so.

The fourth person now put out his head to take a peep, and saw that she was lying down as before; whereupon, not daring to make any noise, he stretched forth his foot and kicked his fellow travlers, who, however, showed no signs of moving.

He now decided to put on his clothes and make a bolt for it, but he had hardly begun to do so before he heard the creaking sound again. Again the dead woman came to him, and, breathing several times on him, went away to lie down as before, as he could tell by the noise of the trestles.

He then put his hand very gently out of bed, and, seizing his trousers, got quickly into them, jumped up with a bound, and rushed out of the place as fast as his legs would carry him. The corpse, too, jumped up, but by this time the traveler had already drawn the bolt, and was outside the door, running along and shrieking at the top of his voice, with the corpse following close behind.

He ran up and thumped with all his might at the gate of a temple. The priest there did not know what to make of it, and would not open to him. The corpse was only a few yards off, he could do nothing but run behind a tree which stood close by, and there shelter himself, dodging to the right as the corpse dodged to the left, and so on. This infuriated the dead woman to madness.

Finally, the traveler escaped, while the corpse remained rigidly doing what it did around the tree. This means his life was saved.

TALE 106

Castration

Ma Wanbao, a scholar in Dongchang, Shandong, was unrestrained. His wife Tianshi was also frivolous, but the couple loved each other dearly.

A lady lodged temporarily at their neighbor's house. The neighbor was an elderly widow. The lady said that she was badly treated by her parents-in-law and therefore was running away from home. She was good at sewing and did some house work for the old widow, who was happy to have her. She declared that she was able to do a form of massage that could cure women of difficult diseases. The old widow often came to visit Ma and his wife, telling them about the young woman and how capable she was. Tianshi listened without really paying much attention.

One day Mr. Ma stole a glance at the lady from a crack in the wall. The lady was about eighteen and very beautiful. Ma became infatuated with her. He formed a plan with his wife. They told the neighbor that Tianshi was sick, hoping to trick the young woman into visiting them. When the old widow arrived, she told Tianshi that the young lady was afraid to meet strange men. "Please ask your husband not to enter the room," she told Tianshi. But Tianshi made excuses, "Our house is small. My husband comes and goes. What can I do?" Then she had an idea, "I'll ask our uncle in Xicun to invite him to dinner. He will be gone all evening. It will be easy." The widow returned home to get the young woman, while the neighbor told her husband about her lies.

That evening, the old widow brought the young girl and asked Tianshi, "Is your husband gone?" Tianshi assured the widow that her husband would be gone all night. "Good!" the girl said. The elderly widow returned to her own home. Tianshi lit a candle and made the bed for the young girl. She let the Girl get into the bed first and then took off her clothes and put out the candle. Suddenly she jumped up. "I forgot to close the kitchen door. The dogs will steal our food if I don't close it." Getting out of bed, she went into the kitchen and let Ma sneak in. Quietly he walked through the dark and climbed into the bed with the young woman. "I have come to cure your disease," the young girl said. Ma kept silent.

The young lady massaged Ma's abdomen and stopped. She reached between his legs and found his penis. The girl was frightened and wanted to run away. She pulled back as if stung by a poisonous snake or scorpion. Ma told her to be still, and reached between her thighs. But he too found a penis where no penis should have been. It was Ma's turn to be shocked. He called for a candle. Tianshi thought her husband's little plot had failed, and she rushed in with a light. The "girl" knelt on the floor, begging for forgiveness. Tianshi was ashamed and frightened. She immediately walked out.

Ma questioned the young man and found out he was Wang Er'xi from Gucheng in Shandong. His elder brother was a disciple of Sang Chong of Lishi County, Shanxi. He had found this way of taking advantage of women by disguising himself as a woman and giving them a "massage". Ma asked him, "How many women have you raped?" Wang Er'xi replied, "I have only slept with sixteen, since I have just learned how to do this."

Ma thought that he should be punished with a life sentence and intended to bring charges against him at court, but he liked the man for his good looks. He decided to mete out his own punishment. He tied the boy's two arms behind him and cut off his penis. The man bled terribly and fainted. He regained consciousness after half an hour. Ma asked him to stay in bed and covered him with a quilt, "I shall treat you with medicine. After you recover, you will stay with me for the rest of your life. Otherwise if I sue you, you will definitely die." Wang Er'xi agreed. The next day, the old widow came. Ma lied to her, saying, "She turned out to be my niece Wang Er'jie. As she is unable to have any children, she was driven out of her home. We realized this after she told us her experience. She is not feeling well at the moment. We want to buy some medicine for her and talk with her husband about keeping her in our house to keep my wife's company." The old lady saw "Wang Er'jie" was pale and sat down beside the bed. "My private parts are swollen," the young boy told the widow. "I am afraid it is a bad sore." The old lady believed this and left.

Ma gave him some medicine and Wang soon recovered. At night they engaged in homosexual pleasures. During the daytime, Wang did the house work for Tianshi as if he were Ma's concubine.

Not long after, Sang Chong was caught and, together with seven disciples, was sentence to death. Only Wang Er'xi escaped death. Still, a warrant for his arrest was issued. The villagers suspected that "Wang Er'jie" was the escaped Wang Er'xi. Old women in the village gathered together to check if the girl was in fact a boy. They felt his private parts through his trousers. But as they felt no male organ, they believed he was truly a she. Wang Er'xi was grateful to Ma and lived with him for the rest of his life. After he died, Wang was buried together with the Ma family west of the town. His tomb can still be found.

TALE   107

Wife and Concubine

Hong Daye was from Jingdu. His wife, Zhu, was a real beauty. The couple seemed to love each other dearly.

Later, Hong Daye took his maid Baodai as his concubine. Although Baodai was not as beautiful as Zhu, Daye loved her and pampered her more than he did his wife. His wife thus grew angry and the couple quarreled bitterly. From that point on, Hong Daye became all the more distant to his wife and closer to his concubine, although he no longer dared to openly sleep in his concubine's room.

The Hongs moved to a new neighborhood and lived next door to a silk businessman whose family name was Di. One day, Di's wife, Hengniang, visited Zhu. Hengniang was in her thirties, with rather ordinary features, and very talkative. Immediately, Zhu found herself enjoying her company. When Zhu visited Hengniang at her home the next day, she found there was also a concubine at the Dis' home. She was a little over twenty and very pretty. After living next door to the Dis for six months, Zhu had heard no complaint from Hengniang. Mr. Di was very much in love with Hengniang and the concubine was a wife only in name.

So one day, Zhu asked Hengniang, "I used to believe that men loved concubines because of what they were. How did you manage it? Please be my teacher and tell me." Hengniang said, "It's you who pulled yourself away from your husband, and yet you complain about men! You quarreled with him, always giving him a dressing down. You were driving him towards his concubine. You were drifting further and further away from him. What you should do for the moment is this, If he comes to you, refuse him. A month later, I'll tell you what to do next." Zhu went home, doing everything to make the concubine look more beautiful and forcing her to keep her husband company during the night. When she and her husband ate together, Zhu would ask the concubine to join them. Whenever Hong Daye wanted to be intimate with Zhu, Zhu refused him so he would have to seek comfort from the concubine. People all praised her as generous and kind.

A month later, Zhu went to see Hengniang again. Hengniang told her, "Go back and change into more shabby clothes. Don't wear any make-up. Wear old shoes. Work at home as if you are one of the maids. Come back again in a month." Zhu went home and did what she was told. Hong Daye took pity on her and told Baodai, the concubine, to help her with her chores. Zhu refused her help.

Another month passed and Zhu went to see Hengniang, who said, "The day after tomorrow is the Spring Outing Festival. I'll take you out. Put on your best clothes and come to me early in the morning." Zhu agreed. On that day, Zhu carefully did her make-up and followed all of Hengniang's instructions. When Hengniang saw her, she was satisfied, only changing Zhu's hairdo so that she looked all the more attractive. Hengniang also redid Zhu's robe to make it more fitting. She took out a pair of shoes that made Zhu's feet more beautiful. That evening, before Zhu went home, Heng-niang also offered Zhu some wine, saying, "Go home and let your husband see you for just a moment. Then shut up your door and sleep. If he comes and knocks at your door, don't open it. Accept him only after he pleads with you three times. Be mean with your tongue, hands and feet when you are together. Return again in two weeks' time." Zhu returned home and let her husband witness her radiant beauty. Hong Daye narrowed his eyes and examined her closely. He seemed happier than he had for some time. Zhu talked a little about her outing, put her hand under her chin as if she were tired. It was not quite dark yet, but she went her room to sleep, shutting her door behind her. A moment later, as expected, Hong Daye came and knocked on the door, but Zhu refused to open it. The next evening, the husband came again and once more was shut out. On the third day, the husband asked his wife why he was always kept out. Zhu said, "I'm accustomed to sleeping alone and do not want to be disturbed." Before sunset that evening, Hong Daye came into Zhu's room, refusing to leave. When they finally were in bed, they were like newly-weds enjoying their honeymoon. When it was over, the husband suggested they do this the following evening. Zhu would not agree, suggesting they go to bed together only once every three days.

Two weeks later, Zhu visited Hengniang, who whispered to her, "From now on, you can have your husband all to yourself. Though you're beautiful, you're not very charming. If you combine a little charm with your natural beauty, you will be unmatched." So Hengniang taught her how to cast eyes at men, telling her, "Your trouble is with your eyes." She also taught her to smile and said, "You're not doing it right. There's something wrong with the left part of your face." She patiently taught Zhu how to charm a man with her eyes and her coy smile. Having studied long and hard under Hengniang, Zhu felt much more confident. Hengniang told her, "Go home and practice in front of a mirror. Success in the wedding bed is something I cannot teach you. You must be flexible, make him happy."

At home, Zhu did as she was taught. Hong Daye was extremely happy and totally captivated by her. His only fear was being rejected by Zhu. Before the sun had set each evening, he was already busy charming and teasing his wife, not leaving her room for one single step. She found it impossible to keep him out of her room now. Zhu was kinder to Baodai, inviting her to join her and her husband for meals. To Daye, Baodai became more and more ugly. He would send her away before the meal was finished. Zhu trapped Daye in Baodai's room and locked the door from outside, but Daye would not even touch Baodai. In the end, Baodai felt insulted and began to speak ill of Daye, which only made Daye more irritated with her. In fact, now he spoke to her primarily through the cracks of whips and switches. Enraged, Baodai stopped worrying about appearances, wearing dirty clothes and shoes and keeping her hair like a heap of grass.

One day, Hengniang asked Zhu, "Did my method work?" Zhu told her, "It has worked beautifully. I have done what you taught me, but I still don't understand the principles. Why did you ask me to let my husband indulge himself in the first place?" Hengniang explained, "Don't you know men love what is new. They love concubines not necessarily because they are beautiful. They love them because they are new, and men like the rare opportunities of having another love. Let them enjoy their concubines to their hearts' content. There is always the time when they are tired of the concubine, no matter how good she is!" Zhu went on asking, "Then why did you tell me first not to wear make-up and to look shabby and later you want me to wear make-up and look attractive?" Hengniang told her, "If you leave something aside without looking at it, soon it will appear as if new. When men suddenly see women with make-up, they seem to have caught their new love. It's like a hungry man suddenly seeing delicious food in front of him, ordinary food immediately becomes tasteless. What you do at this time is not to let your man have you easily. In comparison, Baodai is old and ordinary while you're new. He can easily have her but you are hard to get. This is the method to replace the concubine with the original wife." Zhu was very happy to be told all this and the two women became bosom friends.

One day several years later, Hengniang suddenly said to Zhu, "We've been very close to each other and now there's something I should let you know. I did not tell you before because I was afraid you might be suspicious. Now I'm leaving and I have to let you know the truth, I'm a fox spirit. My mother died when I was very young and my step-mother sold me to Jingdu. My husband was very kind to me and so I could not leave him. I've stayed on until today. But my father will become an immortal tomorrow, and I have to pay him a visit. I won't be able to come back." Zhu held Hengniang's hand, sobbing. The next day, the Dis were in great turmoil as Hengniang suddenly disappeared.

TALE 108

The Rat

During the reign of Wanli of the Ming Dynasty, a rat the size of a cat was found in the palace, posing a great threat. The court solicited from among the people's cats that could catch the super-large rat, but all the cats that had made the attempt were wounded by the rodent beast. Just then a foreign country gave a gift of a beautiful white Persian cat. Palace servants locked it up in the room where the big rat was believed to be making trouble. They hid themselves outside and peeped into the room.

The white cat crouched on the ground for a long while before the rat cunningly came out of its hole. It saw the cat and charged at it. The cat fled to the table, the rat followed and the cat jumped off. This process was repeated no less than a hundred times. People thought that this cat was just another useless coward. Gradually, the rat slowed down, panting for breath and trying to take a rest by lying on the ground. Just then, the cat charged at the rat, biting it on the neck, and the two animals were locked in a fierce fight. When palace servants opened the door and walked in, they found that the rat's head had been bitten into pieces. They realized that the dodging by the cat was not an act of fear, but a tactic with which it waited until the rat had become worn out. To retreat when the enemy advances and to press on when the enemy retreats, this is the right principle.

TALE 109

Shepherd Boys and
the Mother Wolf

Two shepherd boys found a wolf's den with two pups in it. They decided to take one of the little animals each and climbed onto trees some dozen steps apart. Soon the old wolf came back, found her children missing and appeared scared. One shepherd boy pinched the pup's ears and twisted its legs to make it yelp in pain. The old wolf, hearing the cry, rushed to the tree and angrily scratched the tree bark with its paws, howling frantically. Just then the other shepherd boy made his pup cry out. The mother wolf heard the sound, looked around and saw her child. So she ran to this tree, scratching and howling. Just then the pup in the other tree cried out again and the old wolf ran to that tree. Like this, she ran between the two trees several dozen times. Gradually, she slowed down and her crying died out. Finally she was too tired to make a single step and fell down under one of the trees. When the shepherd boys came out of trees, the old wolf was already dead.

Today there are people who act as if they are heroes, putting their hands on their swords, glowering at people as if they are about to gulp down their opponents. Their opponents, however, retreat to their homes and shut the doors behind them. The hero-types scream and swear, and if nobody is bold enough to come out and challenge them, they really feel that they are invincible. They do not know they are just like the wolf in the story and simply are treated as laughing stocks by their opponents.

TALE 110
The Rich Man

One rich man found that people always came to borrow money from him. One day when he went out, a young man followed him. The rich man asked why and was told by the young man that he had come to borrow money from him. The rich man agreed to his request. When they reached home, it happened that several copper coins were lying on the table. The young man stacked them up into several high heaps. Immediately, the rich man refused to lend the money and sent the young man off. Someone asked him why he had done what he did. The rich man replied, "This young man is a regular gambler and not a decent person. So he is very good at piling up the coins as they do in gambling houses. He gave himself away without realizing it." When you come to think of it, there is some truth in what the rich man said.

TALE 111

The Clever Border Commander

Wang Qiyu, from Xincheng in Shandong, served as minister of war in the Ming Dynasty court. When he was commanding the troops on the northern border, he ordered a huge sword built. The blade was more than a foot wide and the whole weapon weighed over a ton. When he toured the border posts, the sword had to be carried by four soldiers. He often deliberately asked people to try to lift the sword and nobody could do it alone. Secretly, Commander Wang had a wooden sword made to the exact measurements. He had the substitute weapon painted silver and often played with it on horseback. When people saw him doing so, they were all scared by his mighty strength.

He also had reeds planted as if they were fences to mark the twisting and turning of the border line. He remarked, "These reeds are my Great Wall!" The Qing troops invaded the border by pulling out the reeds and turning them into ashes. Commander Wang had more reeds planted and they were burned gain. This process repeated itself three times. Finally, Commander Wang had explosives planted beneath the reeds. The Qing troops came to burn the reeds, but triggered the explosives and suffered heavy casualties. Those who were not injured fled. Wang once again had reeds planted. The Qing troops saw the reeds and pulled back. These tactics made Wang a respected person.

Later he retired to his hometown, but soon the situation on the border grew tense again. The court sent for him. Already eighty-three years old, he had to make a great effort to pull himself up from bed to bid goodbye to the emperor who consoled him, "All you have to do is sitting in the command post." So he came to the border and at every border post he visited, he simply slept in the tent. The Qing troops learned that Wang Qiyu was back but could not believe it. Pretending to ask for peace, they came to the Ming barracks to find out whether Wang was indeed back. When they saw Commander Wang lying in bed, safe and sound, they immediately knelt down to show their respect. Then they quietly retreated.

TALE 112

Three Immortals

A student went to Nanjing to take part in the imperial ex-aminations. He passed by Shuqian, where he met three very eloquent scholars. The student bought some wine and drank together with them. The three introduced themselves, one was Jie Qiuheng, another Chang Fenglin and the third Ma Xichi. They drank happily and soon it grew dark. Jie Qiuheng said, "I have not been a very gracious host. My humble house is not far away, you're welcome to stay for the night at my place." Chang and Ma also stood up and they asked the student to take his servant and come along.

On a hill in the north of the town, was a courtyard with a small river winding by. The house was kept very clean. The host asked his servant to light the lamps and look after the servants of the guests. Ma Xichi said, "In the past, scholars made friends by sharing their writings. Now the examinations are coming up and we should make full use of the time tonight. Let's prepare four titles of compositions and write them on small pieces of paper. Through drawing lots, each one of us will pick a title and complete the compositions. After that we'll come and drink together." Everybody agreed and wrote a title. After drawing the subjects, each began to write his composition. At two o'clock in the morning, they finished the articles and shared them. Having read the articles written by the other three scholars, the student was so moved that he copied them down and hid them in his breast pocket. The owner of the house brought out some wine and bid the student drink. Soon he became very drunk. Then the owner took him to another courtyard to sleep. The student was so drunk that he slept with his clothes and shoes on.

By the time he awoke, the sun had already risen. He looked around and did not find any courtyard. He was surprised to find himself and the servant sleeping in a mountain valley. Looking around, he saw a cave and a small river. He checked his pocket and found the three articles still there. He asked the local residents at the foot of the mountain about the cave and learned it was known as the "Three Immortals Cave". The cave provided shelter to three strange animals in the shape of a crab, a snake and a shrimp. They often came out, so the residents saw them now and then.

When the student took part in the imperial exams, he found that the composition titles were identical to those written by the three immortals. His exam scores were of course excellent.